Princess Diana

THE DAY SHE DIDN'T DIE

by

Heath Samples

With

Claire Hooper

Grosvenor House
Publishing Limited

This book is published by
Grosvenor House Publishing Ltd
28-30 High Street, Guildford, Surrey, GU1 3EL.
www.grosvenorhousepublishing.co.uk

A CIP record for this book
is available from the British Library

ISBN 978-1-908596-78-9

Heath Samples LL.B Hons grew up in Scarborough North Yorkshire. After serving in the
Royal Air Force, he studied Law & Economics at University.

He holds a JAR- PPL Private Pilots Licence, RYA Yachtmaster, MCA Boatmasters Commercial Licence and BSAC SCUBA Dive Leader. He has just established and set a brand new Guinness World Record by crossing the English Channel in relay on Sea Scooters.

Foreword

I have realised that life is a series of coincidences that have been strung together by accidents, missed opportunities and actions that have gone very badly wrong. There has never been any room for what some would call fate. That has too much attached to it of an unseen hand guiding our every move. It is here that I would depart from a religious view that God is interested in the minutiae of our lives. Even for an omnipresent, omniscient and all seeing creator, I would dare to say that is a step too far. There must be some things in life that are down to us.

It is all I can get myself to believe that for a lot of the time on this planet we struggle on in our own efforts fulfilling a destiny brought about by our motivation and in many cases desperation.

As I walk through life I have often heard people say.

'What if?'

What if I was late - What if she had not said that - What if that had never happened?

Like a game of chess badly played, we can often look back at the things we have done – or not done and wonder if our destiny would have been very different.

In March 2002 I came downstairs one morning and there and then decided to write a book. I had no notion of what to do and no idea how it could be done. Some desire inside me pushed me on. In a few weeks, a book was completed and in a few months I self-published. That book changed my life. It topped the charts around the world and is now translated into 51 languages. What if I had never wrote it – where would I be today?

It was that question that hung in my mind when I read this book. How would have the world changed if Diana Spencer had not been killed on that fateful night in a tunnel in Paris? At the time of her death she was at the height of her fame. She fulfilled the desires of so many people with her film star looks and exotic lifestyle. Dubbed the Queen of Hearts she touched the lives of millions of people and in an instant her life was ended amongst the stink of blood and gasoline.

Yet, I dare you to imagine what would have happened if they had left the hotel minutes earlier and the crash had not happened. How would her life have changed the world? Imagine if she was pregnant to Dodi and converted to Islam.

Even just thinking these thoughts is enough to start the pulse racing. They are frightening in their consequences and thrilling to just consider. The implications of her surviving that crash are eternal.

To read this book is to ask the vital question - WHAT IF?

For the question to be fully answered our own disbelief in the scenario has to be suspended. Remove from your mind if you can what happened on that fateful day. Allow your imagination to think the impossible – What if Diana had survived?

I can assure you that your time will not be wasted and the story that you are about to read will change the way you look at the world around you.

GP Taylor

New York Times best selling writer.

www.gptaylor.info

Dedication

To my girlfriend Lucy Mollon and my mum
Angela Samples. Without their love,
support and encouragement this book
would not have been possible.

Acknowledgements

I would like to thank Claire Hooper. Her dedication to this book has been outstanding. Her craft is one, which she has truly mastered. Thanks to Demi Quinn at www.copywritingcompany.co.uk for setting me off in the right direction on this journey. Kim Nash who has been a great supporter and invaluable source of information, advice and help at critical times through the books journey and afterwards. Thanks to GP Taylor for his help in getting the book published and avoiding the pitfalls I was about to fall into. To Rick and Steph Lear at Closar Illustration & Design for an outstanding book cover.

My Dad Barry Samples. His support in all the madcap things I do is unfaltering- thanks Dad.

My extended family and friends in Radcliffe on Trent. Thank you all for a great time whilst I was there and also to Allie whose levels of common sense and friendship I can only aspire to.

Thanks also to my steadfast mates Steve Moore, Dan Perkins, Rob Pickering, Tony Ireland, Geoff Bacon, James Newman and Ed Peacock; love you guys! And finally, the Guinness World Record Channel Challenge Team- didn't we do well!

CHAPTER ONE

The click of the door shutting sounds too loud in the silence of the room. Tentatively the couple move forwards, close but not touching. Neither of them makes a sound. She sits on the bed whilst he checks the bathroom, and returns with a cloth to stem the blood from her nose. Her head swims.

They're leaving the restaurant, slipping out of the back to avoid the waiting press. The car is waiting there, the driver holding the door and grinning lazily. The atmosphere is frosty; they're both annoyed that their evening has been ruined. The door slams behind them and the driver accelerates out of the alley, tyres screaming the alert to the waiting press.

The cloth is almost completely red with her blood. She leans forward, pressing it back to her nose while he reaches out and hesitantly strokes her lower back. It is the first time they have touched since it happened, and it does nothing to break their awkward silence. His face is ashen, hers is like chalk. There are no words.

The car races through the back streets of Paris, a little too fast perhaps, but no one shows any concern. There has been a thaw between the couple, they're holding hands and laughing. He leans in to kiss her several times. She is smiling, listening attentively to his stories and laughing in all the right places. The car careers around a corner at speed and the couple laugh as they are thrown together. They kiss before moving back to their seats, still holding hands.

Laughter floats into the room, people returning late from a boozy night out. The couple tense at the sound, not moving until it has disappeared safely into another part of the hotel. The thick carpet in the hall would mask the sound of any approaching footsteps, but they are both listening anyway. Both imagining the worst.

She notices the speed that the car is travelling and looks to the driver for reassurance. His face is tense, his eyes flicking from the road to the rear view mirror and back again every few seconds. Her grip on her lovers hand becomes vice like, drawing his attention. They both glance over their shoulders, taking in the cars hurtling down the road behind them. The drivers hands are clamped down on the steering wheel, the skin straining white across his knuckles. He swerves dangerously into another lane, welcomed by a chorus of angry horns, and pushes the car to go faster, work harder.

He moves his hand from her back and stands up. She raises her eyes to meet his and watches as he begins to pace. It is clear what he is thinking, because the same thoughts are racing through her mind. What really just happened? Who should we talk to? Who can we trust? The stream from her nose seems to have finally stopped, and she slips past him into the bathroom, dropping the blood soaked cloth in the bin on the way. Her reflection glares at her accusingly from the mirror, dried blood smeared in a grotesque goatee across her porcelain skin. She runs the water in the sink and bends down to wash her face. Nausea sears through her and she vomits. Once. Twice. The third time brings up nothing but blood. Drained, physically and emotionally, she collapses on the floor.

Brazenly flouting the speed limit, the car wails through the night time traffic, howls of protest from the other drivers filling the air. The pursuit from behind is relentless, the lights from high powered flashes briefly illuminating the sky. Taking a risk, the driver turns the wheel suddenly into a side street, easing off the accelerator once he sees that they have not been followed. He chuckles to himself once and the atmosphere in the back seat snaps. They all laugh until it hurts, and tears stream from her eyes, lightly smearing her expensive face. The driver eases the car back down to a sensible speed, winding his way carefully through the back streets, before pulling back onto a main road.

She comes round in bed, dressed but beneath the covers. Light streams through the heavy net curtains. Her head throbs and the urge to close her eyes again is overpowering. Still, she raises herself to a sitting position and glances around the room. He is in a chair in the corner, his face buried in his hands. Words still refuse to come, and she watches as he cries in silence.

No one notices the white car at first, all still high on the thrill of freedom. The car edges up slowly, inconspicuous in its ordinariness. It isn't until the first swipe of the drivers side that they even realise that it's there. Edging closer and closer, lights off, the Fiat grinds against the Mercedes paintwork sending up a firework of sparks. The driver panics, his eyes shooting from the road, to the other car, to his passengers. He puts his foot down, confident in the superior size and speed of the car. The Fiat keeps pace, its driver hunched over the wheel, face shrouded in darkness. The cars race, side by side, into darkness.

Someone is banging on the door. A panicked, hurried banging. They're calling out, trying to unlock the door. One of them must have had the good sense to leave the key in it, because no one is getting in. She can hear their names being called, and soon after the phone in the room begins to ring. Neither of them makes a move towards it, but just stare blankly at the intrusive noise. Eventually it stops, and the people at the door move away. She wonders idly if they will come back and break the door down. The image of hotel staff charging in through the door, only to find the two of them sitting there in silence makes her want to giggle. Inappropriate humour. She looks over to him, hoping to catch his eye. With his face still buried in his hands, clearly he is in a different place right now.

The lights in the tunnel are faint, and there is little traffic at this time of night. Side by side the two cars race on, the old white Fiat torturing the sleek new Mercedes mercilessly. Sweat pours from the driver, his hands clamped to the wheel, shaking. The couple are still holding hands, but now it is more for comfort than from affection. They do not speak, do not look at each other, and do not look at the other car. Once again the white Fiat slams into the side of the car, forcing the driver to wrestle heroically to keep it on the road. A tear rolls down his cheek, and unable to raise his hand to wipe it, it drips slowly off of the end of his chin. The full beams from a car travelling in the opposite direction blind them all momentarily, and the synchronised thumping of all their heartbeats seems to vibrate through the vehicle. A squeal like a tortured infant rips through the air. The car jolts. Swerves to the left and slams into a massive concrete pillar.

The phone is ringing again. The shrill noise is sending needles of pain into her brain. They are both aware that at some point they will need to go to the hospital. Need to be checked over. For now, though, neither of them can move. Decisions need to be made. Fears need to be dealt with. Accusations need to be made. He gets up, does not look at her and goes into the bathroom. The door slams behind him.

Everything is still; quiet, like in a dream. There is pain, and blood and the smell of something burnt. Someone is crying. He comes to her, shakes her gently.

"Can you hear me? Are you hurt?"

His voice filled with urgency and concern. She cannot form words, but looks at him and shakes her head.

"We need to get out of here. Can you move?"

She starts to shake her head, but he is already sliding his hands underneath her knees. Flung forward when the car crashed, she is lodged in the foot well, forced into the foetal position. She cries out as he lifts her from the car, wincing but finding she is able to stand as he sets her down. They both look over the wreckage of the Mercedes, frozen in shock at the sight of the driver dead in his seat. The sound of a siren slices through the silence, bringing to life the rest of the night. Several cars race into the tunnel, slowing down to gawp at the accident. The couple look at each other, thinking. Deciding. Holding hands, they slip away from the car and into the darkness of the night.

Tears. The first tears since it happened start flooding down her face. She had been so close to losing everything. So close to leaving her family behind and to giving up on the new life ahead of her, before she had even finished planning it. What began as a silent weeping descends into full blown hysteria as her mind works over the last twelve hours. What went wrong? Someone must have leaked their location to the press, that much was obvious. But how many people knew about the decoy car? And how did the driver of the white car find them when they had managed to lose the rest of their tail? Clearly the agenda of the other driver in the accident wasn't the same as the rest of the paparazzi, so whose agenda was it? Her head begins to swim again as the endless possibilities flit through her mind. Was she being paranoid, or did somebody want one, or both of them, dead? Was he sitting in the bathroom thinking the same thing? Trying to work out which one of them was the intended target, and who could possibly have done this? Flinging the covers off of her legs, she places both feet gingerly on the floor, testing her weight before standing up properly. Shakily, but still able, she moves one foot in front of the other, determined to make it to the bathroom. They will talk. She will tell him her fears and he will make her feel better. He would have a logical explanation for everything, and they would laugh and it would all go away. Keeping her hand trailing along the end of the bed, ready to support her should she need it, she makes her way forwards intent on her goal. Shuffle, shuffle, pause. Shuffle, shuffle, pause. He's still crying, the closed door doing little to mask the pain of his sobs. She reaches the door, her hand outstretched to the knob when the thunder of splitting wood tears into the room. Whack. Whack. Again. He is behind her now, drawn out by the commotion. He snakes his hand around her waist as the door finally gives way to the rain of blows, cracking under the pressure. A man, well dressed, short and bald, flies into the room. Catching sight of the couple standing there he stops dead, relief trickling across his careworn face.

"Diana, Dodi! Thank the heavens, I am so glad you are alright."

CHAPTER TWO

Early as it is, the sun screams down mercilessly. Bright, but not hot. Not yet. The atmosphere as they wait for the members of the press to arrive is tense, filled with many things unsaid. Diana and Dodi had barely left the hotel room before phone calls were being made, a press conference being organised. Neither of them have eaten, or even been to the hospital yet. They have been told that it is more important that the public know that they are ok. More important that the newspapers are mollified, that awkward questions won't be asked. Diana sat patiently while her hair was styled, her makeup applied. Someone had handed her clothes and she had put them on seemingly in a daze, without even bothering to pay attention to what they were. The makeup artist had chattered at her excitedly, explaining that she would only be using minimal makeup on her as she had been told that it would be best if Diana looked a little worse for wear. Play on the public sympathies. She had shrugged and remained detached throughout, most unlike her usual friendly persona. When the makeup artist began work on Dodi Diana stayed close, staring into space like her mind was a million miles away.

Every time a camera clicks Diana jumps a little. Dodi clutches her hand underneath the table, the affectionate gesture hidden away from the press. The waiting journalists scribbled onto their notepads before the questions had even begun, noting down how pale the couple looked, how both their eyes seemed vacant and expressionless. All to add to the drama. All to sell the story. A tall, thin man in an expensive blue suit walks out in front of the waiting press and clears his throat loudly

"As you are aware Diana, Princess of Wales and Dodi Al Fayed were involved in an automobile accident in the early hours of this morning. Conscious of the public's concern for their wellbeing, they have agreed to answer any questions that you may have on this matter, and only this matter."

The threat implicit in his words, the speaker makes his way out of the media glare, handing the reigns over to the press to begin their interrogation. A sea of hands shoots into the air, each one clamouring for attention like a school child. Dodi nods his head vaguely towards the left where most hands are raised and the questioning begins. Where did the accident occur, had either of them sustained any injuries, had they been medically checked over? All standard stuff, all questions that had been expected and an answer had been carefully crafted for each. Where had they been before the accident, what had they done afterwards? Were either of them worried about travelling in a car again? Did they know what had caused the accident? The questions flew across the room like tennis balls, intercepted deftly by either Dodi or Diana, their answer batted back across the room.

"Diana, there are rumours that there was another car involved in the accident?"

The question came right out of left field. A large team of PR and publicists had sent out press releases to all the journalists present advising that the Mercedes had crashed due to an unknown error with the car. Blaming the driver had seemed like an obvious choice, but both Dodi and Diana had been set against it and so the car had been blamed. Sooner or later an accident report would have to be produced to verify this, but for now getting their version of events out there was the main concern.

"I didn't see any other vehicles."

Her eyes dart to the journalist, their bright blue penetrating him as she answered. He held her gaze for a moment before looking down and scribbling something in his notebook. She continues to stare at him while the next question was asked, Dodi nudging her gently to bring her attention back to the matter in hand. He answers the bulk of the following questions, reassuring those gathered there that both he and Diana were shaken but unharmed and sending condolences to the family of the driver killed in the crash. Gathered around them, several news teams transmit the conference live, catching each question and recording every answer the couple give. Dodi speaks eloquently and reassuringly, despite the fact that most questions were aimed at Diana. Her face, frozen into a perfect mask of nothing, continues to scan the assembled crowd. Her eyes dance across the people gathered in front of her, back and forth, back and forth, faster and faster. Underneath the table Diana's hand is still intertwined with Dodi's, clamped together in an almost vice like grip. Every camera is trained on her, every blinding light from a flash aimed in her direction.

The sun bears down even higher in the sky and a trickle of sweat drips down the front of Diana's blouse as the world watches and waits for her to speak. The news teams record every slight move of her head, every blink, every breath, waiting patiently for her to talk again. Still, Diana looks to Dodi to answer for her when a question is asked. Journalists write hurriedly about the effect of the crash on the usually strong, confident woman, using her appearance to lend weight to their story. Stretching the truth to fit the circumstances. True, the skirt and blouse she wears are sombre, plainer than what she was usually pictured in. Her hair, though still impeccably styled, bears the weight of the last twenty four hours of her life. And who wouldn't be pale, have dark circles under their eyes, after being in a car crash? The picture begins to take shape in the minds of the media, the story that had been expertly crafted in the minds of a public relations team. Just another hiccup in the life of the downtrodden Princess of Wales. One more obstacle in her path towards true happiness. Levels of public sympathy will be sky high. The People's Princess triumphing over adversity once again.

"Diana, have you spoken to any other members of the Royal family?"

She had called her sons, of course, before the press conference had taken place. Too young to fully understand what was going on, Diana had explained that she had been in an accident but that she was fine and would be on the news soon just to let everyone know that she was ok. She responds to the question with minimal effort.

"Other than my boys, no."

Every journalists head snaps to attention as they hear her speak. As little as she had said, it was still a direct quote that they could use, and she had given so few of those so far.

"How do you feel about the statement given by Buckingham Palace this morning?"

It is clear by the blank look on Diana's face that she knows nothing about the statement. The journalist probing her tries, and fails to hide his glee at her reaction. Dodi once again steps in on her behalf.

"As I'm sure you can understand it has been quite a busy morning for us..."

He pauses as a chuckle ripples through the crowd

"Neither of us have had a chance to hear the message you mentioned. If you wouldn't mind reading it to us we would be more than happy to comment on it."

All eyes stare at the now slightly flustered reporter as he fishes a crumpled piece of paper out from his notepad and clears his throat. Scratchy with nerves, his voice carries well across the sea of people.

"Since last night's dreadful news there has been an outpouring of concern throughout Britain and around the world, for the health and wellbeing of Diana, Princess of Wales and Dodi Al-Fayed.

We have all been saddened to hear that they had involved in an accident and have waited eagerly for news about their welfare. I know that Diana holds a place in the heart of the country and I am sure that the concern felt by myself and my family is echoed across the nation. Although deeply distraught that the accident occurred, I was relieved to hear that both Diana and Dodi had escaped unharmed. Diana is an exceptional human being who inspires others with her warmth and kindness. Her unwaivering compassion and capacity to smile and laugh would have meant that any injury to her would have been felt in many hearts. I cannot adequately express my relief at her safety and I know that this relief is echoed by the rest of my family, most of all by Diana's sons, William and Harry.

This is also an opportunity for me, on behalf of my family, and especially Prince Charles and William and Harry, to extend the offer of extra security services to Diana in the wake of this disaster. Although an unavoidable accident it is understandable that Diana will be shaken and it is my belief that having increased security around her may go some way to rectify this, as well as offering reassurance to her family.

Our thoughts also go out to the family of the man killed in the crash. I pray that they draw strength from those left around them as they seek to heal their sorrow and then learn to face the future without a loved one.

May those who died rest in peace and may we thank God that both Diana and Dodi are unharmed."

A few seconds pass after he has finished speaking and the words hang in the air like clouds, impossible to see through. People shuffle uncomfortably in the audience as the couple digest the words that had been read out to them. When she speaks, Diana's voice slices through the silence like ice

"I shall be sure to send my thanks to my former family for their concern over my safety and welfare, and politely decline their kind offers of extra security. As we have already stated, this was an unfortunate accident that could not have been avoided."

Although relatively cordial, Diana's tone signals that this will be all she says on the matter, possibly the last she says at all. Pencils scurry across paper as her words are frantically scribbled down, cameras flash repeatedly, each one causing her to flinch slightly. Dodi adds his thanks to the royal family for their kind words, momentarily taking the focus away from Diana and giving her time to compose herself. Her porcelain face has taken on an ashy pallor and tremors rock through both her hands, one still safely entwined with Dodi's. He too looks pale and sleep deprived, the brightness of the day emphasising how much had been taken out of them. Either unusually empathetic or just aware that they had got as much out of the couple as possible, the reporters begin to wind their questions down. Diana still jumps slightly with each click of the camera, however they are becoming fewer and further between. After several moments of heavy silence the man in the blue suit calls out to the press from the wings

"Are there any further questions?"

None apparent, Diana and Dodi rise simultaneously, she fluid and graceful compared to his heavy, lumbered movements. Their hands separate before they will be in view of the cameras, suggesting to those able to see that it was a movement that they had practiced many times before. The cameras once again begin to flash in earnest as the couple walks toward the glossy black cars lined up to take them away. Both Diana and Dodi slow as they approach the cars, glancing at each other for the briefest of moments, before the door is held open for them. Diana tips her fair head and climbs gracefully into the car, followed by Dodi who smiles and waves to the waiting photographers before slamming the door closed behind him. As the car begins to pull away the couple once again reach for each other's hands, away from the prying eyes of the press. Instructed to take them to the hospital for the check up they had both claimed to already have had, the driver weaves artfully through the London traffic, stopping only at red lights. Diana and Dodi smile and wave to other drivers and pedestrians who look into the car, thrilled to be able to say they have seen a celebrity. The smiles, though wide, never seem to quite reach their eyes. As the car speeds off through the final set of lights before arriving at the hospital a small silver car squeals in exertion as it attempts to overtake.

Cursing, the driver slows, allowing the silver car to pass, too busy to notice that both of his passengers have turned a disturbing shade of grey. Dodi places his arm gently around Diana, part comforting gesture, part to try to halt the tremors which had started earlier in her hand and were now charging through her whole body. Delivered to the hospital via a discreet side entrance, it takes Dodi and two nurses to remove Diana from the back of the car. Gripping her arms and encouraging her to breathe deeply, they don't even flinch as she vomits violently on the pavement twice, before being helped into the sterile corridor of the hospital.

CHAPTER THREE

Oh my God. Even though it's on the TV, on the news and everything, I still can't believe it. I must look like a fish, staring at the screen open mouthed, waiting for it all to sink in. Still, I must look better than she does though. Diana is as white as a sheet, and Dodi doesn't look much better either. It was my Mum who phoned me, told me to turn the TV on. She didn't say anything else, just "Ella, turn on the TV" and then she was gone. I thought it was going to be the start of World War Three or something, until I heard the reporter mention something about Diana, Princess of Wales.

I was four years old and I desperately wanted my Mum to play princesses with me in the back garden. She told me I had to wait because she was busy. It looked to me like she was watching something on the TV. I was just about to throw the biggest strop when I saw her. A real princess, in a big white dress, getting married to an actual prince. I was hooked. I sat down next to my mum and we watched the whole thing together. Occasionally she'd point out someone famous in the background, but mostly we just sat in silence. And that was it. Once I was old enough to realise that I was never actually going to be a princess I contented myself with following Princess Diana's life. What she was wearing, who she was spending time with, the charities she was involved with. I remember sobbing for hours when I was about six because my mum wouldn't agree to let me dye my mousy hair blonde. People have said I look like her actually. When she was younger, anyway. I dyed my hair as soon as I was old enough to do it myself, and even Mum had to admit how nice it looked once she was done yelling at me. I keep my hair short like hers too, and try to dress like her. She always looks so elegant, so chic. It's hard to achieve a look like that on a student budget, but I like to think I don't do bad. Maybe one day I'll land a prince of my own, although round here that's not likely. I don't think that marrying Charles was what made Diana a princess though. What most people love about her is more to do with the type of person she is.

There have been a lot of photos of Diana and Dodi in the papers over the last couple of weeks, lots of speculation about their relationship. I reckon it's pretty serious if she took her boys on holiday with him though. I mean, no one introduces their kids to someone unless they think it's going to be serious, even if that someone is a family friend. Plus, she always looks so happy in the candid shots that the photographers have managed to catch. When she knows they are there she wears the same sensible, dignified face expected of her, but on the rare occasions she is caught unaware the pictures have been breathtaking in their joy. Really relaxed, happiness just seems to radiate from her. Not since the photos of her before, during and maybe just after her wedding has she looked so full of bliss. Even then it was more of an uptight bliss. You could see it in her face, the constant fear of doing something wrong. She was never going to be good enough for them though, never going to be the right sort of person. I was devastated when Charles and Diana split up, I think I cried for a week, and moped for a few more. I thought the fairytale was over, that there was no hope for anyone if Charles and Diana couldn't make it work. For months I even thought it was inevitable that my parents were going to break up, because that's what couples did. It wasn't until I was much older that I understood that royal marriages were much more complicated than normal ones and that Charles and Diana had married more out of obligation than actual love. Even just from what came out in the press about their relationship it was easy to see that it must have been hell, probably for both of them, although I've never had much sympathy for Charles. I can't imagine all of the things that were hushed up, although that Panorama interview was enlightening. I bet she got hell for doing that. That was another thing we watched together, me and Mum. We sat down on the sofa with a box of chocolates that we never opened because we were too riveted to the screen. I don't think anyone had any idea that she would say that much, that she would be so open, so honest. Diana came across as honestly devastated at the failure of her marriage and heartbroken at what she saw as her family's attempts to ruin her public image. There was stuff in the papers later claiming that the interview was just an attempt to discredit Charles and the rest of the Royal family, but even if it was who could blame her? Diana clearly felt abandoned, victimised and seriously let down. The interview might not have been in the best taste, but it must have been refreshing for her to finally get her story told, to feel as if she had some control over the course of her life. And the things she said! To lay yourself bare like that for the whole world to see really took some guts. Every single fault that Diana saw in herself she admitted to. Every tiny little problem, every personality flaw she stood up and faced. It must have broken her heart to know that her husband was having an affair, made her feel useless and inadequate. To share that with an entire nation of people must have taken a lot of courage. A lot of women would have had trouble even admitting it to themselves. She's a strong woman though, I think that's some of her problem. The rest of the world might have moved on, but it seems like upper class women are still stuck in the past. They should be seen and not heard, there to adorn their husbands arm. Diana was never going to be that kind of woman. Diana was never really going to fit in.

I still can't work out what I think of her and Dodi as a couple though. They do both look very happy together, most of the time. It's not really fair to try and judge them on their happiness hours after they've been in a car crash I suppose, but most of the pictures of them together show them looking very happy. Still, it can't be easy being from such different backgrounds. I wonder what my parents would say if I came home with a Muslim man? I'd like to think they'd be understanding, but you never know. And that's family. I wonder how the rest of the world would be? A normal person might get comments in the street or funny looks on the bus, but when you're in the public eye you get every inch of your personal life written about, dissected, by the newspapers. It's got to be tough on any relationship. He's quite a good looking man though, in his own way I suppose. And he's used to a life in the public eye. Plus he's got plenty of his own money so he's clearly not after hers. Maybe years in the same social circles has given them enough in common that their different backgrounds aren't so much of a problem.

Maybe it's true that nothing can get in the way of real love. Time will tell I suppose. She looks very grateful to him for being there though, at the press conference. Got to feel a bit sorry for him really. Outside of his family, no one really cares that Dodi was even in the crash. It's all about her. He's handling the press like a pro though, working the crowd, trying to make them not notice that it's him doing all of the talking, giving all the answers. They're not buying it at all, but it's a nice attempt. You can tell Diana is grateful for it too. Bless her, she looks like she has been knocked sideways by the whole thing. Even though her hair is perfect and her clothes are immaculate, if a little subdued, there's something missing. Her usual sparkle, the smile that seems so genuine all of the time, is missing. Her blue eyes seem mostly vacant, except for a few times when the journalists asked awkward questions. The official statement from Buckingham Palace said everything that it was supposed to say, but you could tell from the look on Diana's face that she didn't believe a word of it. Still, she played her part too, gave the response that was expected of her. And there was that moment that that old journalist asked her about another car being involved in the crash. I thought her eyes were going to burn holes right through him. I suppose it was just the annoyance of not being listened to, repeating yourself again and again. It must get pretty tiring, frustrating, being asked the same question again and again. And trying to talk about one thing when all people are interested in is something else. Usually Diana plays the game with the press well, they love her, and she plays to them. Today she clearly hasn't got the patience for ridiculous questions. I mean, if there was another car involved in the crash everyone would know about it.

Pictures of the crash are already being shown and there is clearly only one car there. The other party would have hung around to share insurance details, wait for the ambulance and make sure everyone was ok. Unless they weren't insured or something, but then why would Diana's team be covering up for them? It's impossible to imagine that someone could crash into a car like that and just speed away. It would be obvious that someone important was in the car, most people would keep their distance. Unless it was the press, trying to get one more photo. But again, why would they be covering up for them? No, that journalist clearly needs to check his facts, think before he opens his mouth.

The press conference is drawing to a close on the screen, which is a good job. My legs have gone numb from sitting on them and my eyes are beginning to hurt from staring at the screen. Diana and Dodi stand together as the questions finish and are assaulted by a wave of flashes. She flinches visibly and I feel a surge of sympathy for her. Clearly life in the media isn't easy. The world wants reassuring that she's ok and she's supposed to smile and put on a brave face for them, but who's reassuring her? God, she looks pale and drawn. They're ushering her towards a sleek black car like it's the most normal thing in the world. Who thought that would be a good idea? If it was me I'd be terrified to get in a car ever again. The pair of them only pause for a second though, before ducking into the car and closing the door firmly behind them. The TV flicks back to the newsreader with the bad perm and too much makeup and I switch off. I'm not interested in what she's got to say. I can't stop thinking about Diana. What must have been going through her mind when the car crashed? It shows that it doesn't matter how famous you are, how much money you have, anything can still happen to you. I reach out to the phone, about to dial my mum, when it rings. Clearly Mum had the same idea, phoning to check I'm ok. I pretend to be embarrassed, point out that I'm a grown woman and that she only spoke to me half an hour ago. I'm not about to admit to her that I was just about to do the same thing. We talk about the press conference for a bit, just small talk really. Mum seems as shocked by the whole thing as I am. Really makes you think about how things can change so quickly. Anything could have happened, I mean, what if Diana had died?

Chapter Four

The ring sparkles in the sunlight, hundreds of tiny diamonds sending showers of light across the room. Diana holds the chunky piece of jewellery in the palm of her hand, as if afraid to hold it any closer. She had been searching amongst his things for a piece of paper, something so irrelevant its quest was immediately abandoned upon discovery of the ring. So different from the last ring a man had given her, Diana tentatively examines the heavy ring, admiring the rectangular diamond at the centre surrounded by a stunning gold star. She holds it up to the light, before tentatively slipping it on to her forth finger on her right hand. Arm extended in front of her, Diana admires the look of the solid ring on her delicate hand, too absorbed to hear Dodi entering the room

"It's supposed to go on the other hand...."

He lets the statement hang in the air as Diana's ice blue eyes meet his deep brown ones, shock evident in them. He crosses the room to her, his long strides eating up the distance and takes both of her hands in his.

"I bought that on the night of the accident. I'd been intending to give it to you soon, to ask you soon."

A flush creeps over Dodi's face and the words fall over themselves as they struggle out of his mouth. Diana's face stays blank although she doesn't remove her hand from his. For a few seconds neither of them speak, the silence heavy between them. Diana looks to the ground and clears her throat delicately before speaking.

"I don't understand. Ask me what?"

As she looks up a teasing smile crosses her face causing Dodi to groan theatrically.

"You're going to make me do it properly, aren't you?"

His deep voice betraying just a hint of laughter at the look on her face, he sinks to one knee before Diana. Breathing deeply, suddenly all of the laugher is gone from the room as he looks up at her pale face and bright shining eyes. The smirk wiped from her face, she stares down at Dodi as he breathes deeply before speaking

"Diana, will you marry me?"

She opens her mouth to reply, but the words seem to catch in her throat. The most she can manage is to nod her head, eyes filling with tears as Dodi slips the ring off of her right hand and on to her left. The couple stand together and embrace briefly, before stepping apart. Diana slips the ring from off of her finger and hands it back to Dodi for safekeeping. Something unspoken passes between them, knowledge gleaned from years of living their lives in the public eye. There are PR people that need to be consulted before Diana can be seen out in public wearing an engagement ring, the press must be informed at exactly the right moment.

"I need to speak to William and Harry."

Diana smiles at Dodi and slips her hand into his, squeezing gently. He smiles back at her widely, before leaning in to kiss her softly, his large hands gently cupping her delicate face.

A hint of a smile dances at Diana's lips as she follows the nurse around the ward. At each bed she sits with the patient, chatting softly about their lives, their illness and their hopes for the future. Her smiles are warm and genuine; her laugh comes freely as if she is already close friends with each person she speaks to. She drapes herself casually over plastic chairs, seemingly without a care for her expensive pastel suit. The pearls at her ears and neck shine softly in the dull florescent lights, her teeth catching the same light with every flash of her smile. The drive to the hospital had been uneventful, although Diana had made sure her seat belt was firmly fastened, checking it several times. Her delicate hands had gripped the leather of the seat, her knuckles turning white. Once the car had stopped, she had waited for the door to be opened and had exited with her usual poise, waving genially to the people and press gathered. Unusually, she had not stopped to talk, making her way into the hospital as quickly as possible. Always keen to talk, today she had spent especially long with each person, or lingering beside their bedside as if she was trying to drag out the engagement as long as possible. When there were no more possible people to talk to, no more wards to visit, Diana made her way towards the waiting press to talk about her work with the hospital.

She moves through her speech mechanically, her eyes either lowered or darting across the assembled crowd. As several members of the press raise their hands and shouted questions begin to fill the air, Diana moves away from the crowd, her security team following closely behind her. They weave through the corridors at a steady speed, as if eager to put as much distance between Diana and the press as possible. Her footsteps falter as she reaches the exit and the bright sunlight blinds her momentarily. In front of the building waits a black Mercedes, the driver standing expectantly at the passenger door. Diana's eyes widen, her gaze taking in her security team, the black car and the road in front of her. She seems frozen to the spot, unable to take the steps required of her. Several pairs of eyes bore into her, waiting for her to do something. Finally Diana takes a step forward, smiling weakly at the driver holding the door open for her. She visibly shakes as she slides into her seat, her eyes still flicking across her surroundings and jumping as the door slams behind her. She buckles her seat belt as the engine starts, her hands shaking so badly it takes her several attempts to make the connection. Her blue eyes stare glassily ahead as the car pulls out into the traffic, the driver manoeuvring easily amongst the other cars. Her breaths are deep, audible in the quiet of the car and more than once the driver stares worriedly at her in the rear view mirror. Pale and vacant, Diana seems lost in her own world for the entire journey.

When the car finally stops, Diana is pulled from her reverie only by the sound of the door being opened. Her eyes are wide with fright and it takes several seconds for her to realise where she is. The steps to her expensive Kensington home are just a few feet in front of her and the driver of the car is giving her the same concerned look he has been perfecting all afternoon. Ignoring his gaze, Diana swings her legs out of the car and moves gracefully towards her own front door, stepping through as it is opened from the inside. Diana sighs loudly, all the breath exhaling from her body as the door is closed behind her, shutting out the outside world.

Ignoring the few members of staff gathered at the bottom of the stairs, Diana makes her way to her bedroom, her sanctuary. Closing her eyes, she leans against the door briefly, her body seeming to relax slightly in the process. Her handbag falls to the floor and she slips her feet out from her shoes, sliding her tight clad feet onto the thick cream carpet. Opening her eyes, Diana surveys the room, travelling slowly from one corner to the next and back again. The bed, perfectly made up with heavy cotton sheets, has been changed since this morning when she left. The door to the bathroom is slightly ajar, light from the windows spilling out into the room. She steps forward slowly, her feet sinking into the luxurious carpet and trails a hand across the furniture. First the dresser, then on to the bed and finally finishing at the wardrobe. Peering into the bathroom, Diana scans the rows of toiletries and cosmetics lined up beneath the mirror, the soft towels folded neatly on the edge of the bath. She stays transfixed for a few moments, before closing the door and wandering towards the bed. Climbing on, Diana rests her blonde hair gently on the pillows adorning the head of the bed, turns to her left and brings her knees in close to her chest. Her bright blue eyes remain firmly open as she stares into space, curled up in the foetal position. Silence dominates the house, no noise except for the occasional tweet from a bird outside, the staff going about their business as noiselessly as possible. Twice in the time she lay there the telephone rang downstairs and shortly after a quiet knock was heard on her bedroom door. The knock was not repeated when she does not respond, and Diana makes no move to find out who the caller had been. As the day wears on the light from the windows begins to darken, but still Diana does not move. She does not eat, nor go to the bathroom or make any attempt to remove the expensive suit that she had curled up in whilst still wearing. Occasionally pools of tears would fill in her eyes, threatening to spill over, although they never did.

It is gone midnight when Dodi finds her, still curled up in the foetal position. They had been supposed to meet for dinner but Diana had not turned up. Downstairs her driver had apologised profusely, but when Diana had not turned up for the car and there had been no reply from her room he had presumed that his services were not required. Dodi hadn't bothered to respond, heading straight upstairs to check Diana's room. She hadn't noticed him for almost a full minute, still lost in her own thoughts. It is only when he sits down on the bed next to her, blocking her line of view that their eyes finally meet. The cornflower blue of Diana's eyes swim with unshed tears and the instant Dodi takes her hand they finally spill over. Without speaking, he wraps his arms around her, pulling her head into his lap and holds her while sobs rack through her body. Silently, several tears slide down his dark cheeks, dripping onto Diana's crumpled suit. Her usually perfectly styled hair is dishevelled, matted close to her head on one side. Make up courses down her face, black rivers lining her cheeks.

They stayed like that until morning, neither of them sleeping. Neither of them speaking. Once Diana's tears had run dry Dodi had moved himself behind her, tucking her body tight against his. At first light she rose from the bed, unwinding Dodi's arm from around her and made her way into the bathroom. While she showered, Dodi moved from the bed, almost tripping over the shoes that he had discarded at the foot of the bed halfway through the night. When Diana emerges from the bathroom some half an hour later she finds him still staring aimlessly, having moved from the bed to the window. His dark eyes are fixed across the lightening landscape, vacant, creases etched deep into his forehead. Diana stands behind him silently for a moment, before pressing her still damp form against his back and struggling to wrap her arms around his waist. Both of them have engagements today, meetings that need to be attended, public appearances that need to be made. It is a few hours still until the public persona needs to be adopted, before real feelings need to be locked away. It is still a few hours before they both need to go about their business pretending that all is right with the world, that everything is the same as it always has been.

CHAPTER FIVE

"Thank you, you may leave us."

Diana takes the unusual step of escorting the maid to the door and closing it behind her. She waits a few seconds, listening intently, before returning to her seat and picking up the delicate bone china cup. William and Harry stare at her, waiting for her to say something. She places the cup back down on the saucer, her hand shaking and the faint *ching* echoing across the near silent room. Harry rubs his shoes together awkwardly, a faint squeak emitting from the highly polished leather, before his brother nudges him sharply in the ribs.

"Stop it."

William's voice catches Diana's attention and she raises her head to meet his gaze, their features almost mirrored in each other. They had only returned from Balmoral that very morning and both boys eyes were heavy with tiredness. William sweeps his hand across his heavy sandy hair, pushing it back from his forehead and letting it fall back into place. Harry continues to stare at his own image reflected back in his shiny shoes, pulling faces when he thinks no one can see. Diana shifts uncomfortably in her seat and reaches for her tea again, before changing her mind. They boys had already filled her in on their time with their father, their activities at

Balmoral. Now it was clear that there was something that Diana needs to say, but seems unable to form the words. Both boys had practically flown into her arms upon seeing her, their close bond emphasised by their time apart and their concern for their mother's safety. Although she had reassured them repeatedly that she was fine, both Harry and William had seemed pleased to be able to verify for themselves that this was true. Diana clears her throat, her words coming out small and faint.

"Dodi has asked me to marry him."

Harry's head snaps up, his eyes searching his mothers face. His freckled complexion pales, his ginger eyebrows arch. William breaths deeply, keeping his face blank and calm. Diana's eyes bore into her sons, seeming to search for the emotions her revelations has caused. It is William who breaks the silence

"I suppose we're not surprised really, not after the holiday.'

"Did you say yes?"

Harry jumps in, speaking over the top of his brother in an effort to get the words out.

"Harry, please, wait for your brother to finish speaking. I said a provisional yes, until I had spoken to you. I don't want you to feel unhappy or uncomfortable in any way."

The room stays silent for several minutes, William and Harry taking time to consider their mothers words.

"As long as you're happy, then we're happy."

William again speaks for his younger brother

"It's not as if Dodi is a stranger or anything, and you're happy when you're with him. If you want to marry him then I think you should."

Harry smiles weakly and nods, agreeing with his older brother. It takes him a few minutes, but when he finally manages to speak he has a few questions.

"Will you be moving to live with him? Or will he be moving here? Have you told Father? Will you be changing your name? Are you going to have a baby together?"

Diana seems momentarily overwhelmed by all the questions and takes a moment to gather her thoughts before speaking, answering his questions in a different order to the one he asked them

"You boys are the first people I have discussed this with. Your opinion is the most important to me. I haven't spoken to either your Father or your Grandmother in regards to this, so I would appreciate it if you didn't mention it either. Dodi and I haven't discussed our future plans any further than the possibility of us getting married, but I promise you that you will both be consulted about any decisions that are made."

Harry's face relaxes as he takes in his mother's words and William smiles easily at both of them. Diana takes a sip of lukewarm tea and grimaces slightly at the taste, before placing her teacup back on the saucer on the tray in front of her.

"So when are you telling everyone?"

This time it is Harry who speaks, his mind working over the complexities of the situation.

"I suppose the next step is to speak to the PR team, see when they think the best time to make the announcement is."

Diana's voice sounds heavy with the concerns of obligation.

"And what about Father? Are you going to tell him yourself?"

"I don't think that your Father, or Camilla, are particularly concerned with me now that we are no longer married."

The boys shift uncomfortably on the sofa and avoid their mothers eye, as if it is a subject they are not keen to talk about. Diana seems to sense their discomfort and hastily changes the subject.

"Back to school next week, are you excited?"

She smiles broadly at their exaggerated chorus of groans.

Every newspaper's headline are variations of the same few words, pictures of Dodi and Diana smiling broadly printed on every front page. The Telegraph and The Mail both feature enlarged photographs of Diana's new engagement ring, comparing the chunky form with the daintier piece given to her by Charles. The public relations team that Diana and Dodi consulted with had been keen for them to share their news as soon as possible, in order to give the public something else to focus on other than the accident in Paris. Several well known comedians had been making jokes about the accident and a few of the lower ended tabloids had alluded to the idea that the accident might have been something far more sinister. Keen to counteract the negative press, Diana and Dodi had found themselves standing on the steps of her Knightsbridge home smiling and showing off her ring to the assembled media, Diana squeezing Dodi's hand so tightly that her knuckles turned white.

They gathered together the papers the following morning over breakfast and, taking half each, they began to read through what had been written about their announcement. They chat and laugh while eating, comparing which pictures have been used of them and what angle each different paper has taken. Some have looked at Diana's last marriage and made comparisons between Charles and Dodi, some have began speculating when and where the marriage will take place and some of the cheaper newspapers have already began planning the public celebrations. Diana and Dodi smile at each other as they read through the stories, pointing out things that make them smile. As they finish eating, the pair walk to the front door holding hands and share a quick kiss before they leave the house. As soon as the front door is opened they are bombarded with a stream of flashes from the crowd of photographers gathered at Diana's gate. Clearly panicked, Diana steps back from the door, slamming it hard against the hoard gathered out there. Breathing deeply Diana looks to Dodi, his face pinched together in worry. Her breathing slows and she looks up at him, slightly abashed, and offers a small smile. He reaches out for her hand and together they open the door once more and wave and smile for the crowd gathered at the gate. Not just media, some well wishers had come to wave at the couple and call out their best wishes. Diana's rigid stance relaxes a little and her smile warms as she spends several minutes waving and smiling for the cameras.

The barrage of questions and flashes continues as the couple begin to descend the steps and make their way to the respective cars waiting for them. Diana has eschewed the traditional black Mercedes as much as possible over the last few weeks, instead opting for a large Range Rover to carry her to her official engagements. Its tyres crunch noisily over the gravel driveway, drowning out the noise of people calling her name as she passes. Although slightly more relaxed in this vehicle, she still checks her seatbelt several times before they have even left the driveway and stares forlornly out of the window as she watches Dodi clamber into the standard issue Mercedes waiting to take him to his daily meetings. As the car swings past the photographers, still clicking away furiously, Diana's eyes widen as she scans the crowd intently. On photographer pushes to the front of the crowd, his camera held above his head, and charges out in front of the car. His camera flashing furiously, he recklessly hurls himself towards the vehicle. The driver curses loudly and swerves the car violently out of the way, mounting the curb slightly in the process. Regaining his composure, the driver looks apologetically into the rear view mirror, and taking in Diana's pale face and clenched fists, offers a few words of apology. Leaning forward, Diana meets his eye in the mirror and states calmly

"If that happens again, don't bother to swerve."

He stares back at her for a moment before chuckling softly to himself and turning his eyes back to the road ahead.

The day has been long, filled with endless questions, mostly about the engagement. Diana had smiled politely and tried to be as friendly as possible, showing people her ring and talking about Dodi and explaining that they had made no plans as yet. Everyone she spoke to seemed to have their own ideas about where she would marry and how soon it would be. Several people even asked about her dress and who she was thinking of having as her bridesmaids. As politely as possible Diana had repeated that they had made no plans yet, and had tried to focus on the matter at hand. Her visits to the hospice were usually sombre, but even patients dying from AIDS usually keen to simply talk quietly and enjoy time with Diana wanted to discuss her recent news. Doctors and nurses just passing by had stopped to congratulate her. By mid afternoon Diana was starting to look pale and her smile had begun to wane each time the engagement or upcoming wedding was mentioned. She had posed for photographs with some of the patients, having allowed only one handpicked photographer to accompany her on her round. Several times Diana had to be prompted to remember to smile, or reminded of a pose she had made hundreds of times before. Shaking hands with one of the doctors Diana had handed over a cheque for the hospice, part of the reason for her visit. Her speech, when she made it, was quiet, several times Diana seemed to lose track of what she was saying and twice she had to look at the cheque to remember the amount which had been donated. Clearly not at her best, Diana made her excuses as early as possible, apologising and blaming a headache for her untimely departure.

Again assaulted by a barrage of photographers as she leaves the hospice, Diana shields her eyes and tries to walk with some dignity towards the waiting four by four. Stumbling over a loose flagstone on the pavement, the camera flashes go into overdrive as Diana trips and is caught at the last minute by one of her security team. Red in the face, she attempts to smile for the cameras and laugh off the incident, but her eyes fill with tears. Turning back towards the car, she relies still on her bodyguards arm to make the ascent into the car and waits for him to slam the door behind her. Once again the cameras begin to flash as the car moves out into the traffic, Diana staring vacantly out of the window.

CHAPTER SIX

A wedding. Another wedding. I mean, I know it won't be the same as the last one, but it's still a wedding. I heard it on the news, saw Diana and Dodi standing in front of a crowd of photographers showing off her ring. It couldn't be more different to her last one, but I kind of like that. Completely new man, completely new start, completely new life. I cut out the pictures from all the magazines and newspapers I could find, put them together in a little book I've started on the wedding. A couple of the newspapers have already started talking about the venue and the guest list. Personally I reckon she'll want to do it low key, on a beach somewhere maybe, but I've cut out and stuck in all their ideas. Same with dresses and guest lists. One glossy magazine had a huge feature about wedding dresses two days after the announcement, fashionable designers and high street brands. I think even Diana's dress will be low key. Elegant, but not high street. As if Diana would wear something off of the high street. I'm thinking it'll be like a simple sheath dress, in cream or ivory. Something classic, that shows off her figure. She always looks elegant. I loved her dress when she married Charles, but I was four and that was the eighties. I think definitely less meringue and more class. Plus I wouldn't think that this wedding will be a televised event watched by millions and attended by thousands of people. Knowing Diana and Dodi they probably want to keep it as private as possible, to keep the press away. I wouldn't be surprised if they even tried to slope off and do it on the quiet. I know I would if I were in their situation. I mean, who really wants to spend their whole life practically stalked? I really felt for Diana when that picture of her almost tripping outside that hospice was printed. You could tell from the look on her face that she was close to tears. Who really wants to spend the happiest day of their life looking over their shoulder to make sure no one is watching who shouldn't be? You're supposed to pay photographers to capture the beauty of your wedding day, not have them hound you so they can try and sell your privacy to the highest bidder.

In every newspaper there is something different every day. Some tabloid tale of how so and so doesn't approve of the engagement, how this friend of Dodi doesn't get on with Diana's third cousin once removed and how this might interfere with the seating plan. I'm cutting them all out. One newspaper even speculated about which of the royals might be attending. Surely it's not just me who thinks it weird that people would even consider inviting the family of their ex husband to their next wedding? Although I suppose Charles is pretty much with Camilla now, and at least publically everyone pretends to be sociable. Still, I think it would be weird if any of them were there. I mean, what would they say to each other? Sorry it didn't work out first time round, better luck this time? You can tell none of them really approve of Diana and the way she lives her life. I always think it's so petty when parents get involved in break ups, take sides. I guess it must be pretty different for such a high profile couple and a family so desperate to maintain a good public image. On paper Diana must have seemed like a dream come true, what with how the public took to her. Mum always said that she made the Royal family seem more human for a while, until the divorce anyway. Until all the stuff came out about Charles' affair and Diana's eating disorder, self harming and suicide attempts. He'd been one half of the country's darling couple and practically overnight he was being viewed as a monster. I suppose you can understand why the Queen is a bit pissed. Even though both Diana and Charles admitted to being unfaithful during their marriage, there is something about Diana that just screams vulnerability. I felt sorry for her when I heard her talk about cheating on Charles. I was livid when I found out that he'd cheated on her. In the long run I think the admission did him some good, to be seen holding his hands up and admitting that he was wrong. It's not often that someone in the public eye does that, especially a Royal. Still, he seems too stuffy and reserved, compared to Diana's warmth and openness. That Camilla seems just like him. Maybe that's the attraction. She's no looker, especially not compared to Diana. Not that they're an official couple. Not yet, anyway. I bet the news of the engagement isn't particularly welcomed by any member of the Royal family. Instead of keeping a low profile, Diana has kept up her charity work and is now engaged to another high profile man who couldn't be more different from Charles. I wonder how they feel about the fact that Diana is marrying a man of a different race, a different religion?

I wonder how that works, having a wedding where the bride and groom are two different religions. Do they have one ceremony each? Or compromise somewhere in the middle? It's not something I've ever really thought about before, maybe they haven't either. I mean, it's not even like they're two different denominations of the same religion. Is a Muslim even allowed to marry a Christian? Or a Christian allowed to marry a Muslim for that matter? I suppose they must be or Dodi wouldn't have proposed. Unless he doesn't know. But isn't being super religious and knowing all of the rules part of being a Muslim? It's not like Christianity, where loads of people say they're Christian but pick and choose which rules to follow. My Mum used to say that going to church doesn't make you any more Christian than standing in a garage makes you a car. Most people I know who say they're Christian don't go to church at all, but I'm sure going to the mosque weekly is part of being a Muslim too. So I suppose Dodi would know all about what he is and isn't allowed to do. It's like a community isn't it? They all look out for each other? So even if Dodi was doing something that was frowned upon, you would think that someone would tell him. Or his parents would have advised him against it. Maybe they did though and Dodi just ignored it. There are a couple of Muslim guys at uni, different courses mind, but they're pretty hard workers. Never see them out and about getting drunk, or even socialising that much. Definitely never seen any of them with a girl. I sat next to one of them on the train coming home one time and it was a struggle to get more than a few words out of him in the whole three hours. He just looked at his books, and when he got off the train I saw his mum and dad waiting on the platform for him. Who does that to a kid once they've left home and gone to university?

It has been in the paper this week that apparently not everyone is happy about the news of the engagement.

There was an anonymous letter printed in one of them, I forget which, claiming that Diana wasn't the right sort of woman to be a wife to a Muslim man and that Dodi should reconsider his proposal. I hate people like that. I suppose there are nosy people who like to give their opinion on everything, but writing to a newspaper to have your two pence worth about a relationship between two people you've never met. Who do these people think they are? It must be so difficult to live your life with the world watching, although Diana seems to make a pretty good job of it. To continually smile and chat with the press after all that has been written about her and after being practically stalked for the last fifteen or so years. I don't know that I'd be so patient. I definitely don't think I'd be able to keep living my life the way I want to without worrying what people are going to say and write about me. Clearly it doesn't bother Diana though, or she wouldn't be marrying Dodi. I mean, after Charles he wasn't exactly what was expected of her. Maybe that's part of the appeal though. Like she said in that interview, she spent so long trying to conform and be what she was supposed to be. It's probably quite liberating to do as she pleases, make whatever choices she likes. She's a bit older and a bit wiser this time round, used to dealing with a high profile and not blinded by the glitz and glamour of the life being offered to her. I think that she knows herself a bit better too, Mum says that it's only through adversity that we learn about ourselves, so I guess Diana must know herself inside and out.

I wonder if they'll have a long engagement or if the wedding will be soon? I don't think the press will be able to hold out this level of coverage for months, although stranger things have happened. I imagine William and

Harry will both be involved in the wedding somehow, maybe Diana will get William to give her away, or have Harry do a reading. They're too old to be pageboys, but I would think Diana would want them to play a part in some way. Depends on how they feel about the wedding though I suppose. If they're not one hundred percent behind it then they might not want to be involved. Diana and Dodi said in their statement to the press that the boys were pleased for them, but you never know how much truth is in those statements. Things would certainly be much more interesting if people could always just say what they mean, although it's all part of being in the public eye I suppose. She looked lovely in all the pictures though, really relaxed and genuinely happy. The ring isn't what I'd have picked, looks a bit chunky on her delicate little hand, but she looked proud when she was holding it up to the camera. I think picking an engagement ring is a pretty hard job for a man in all honesty. It's something your wife is going to wear for the rest of her life, if you don't know her well enough to pick something she likes are you sure you know her well enough to marry her? I think the ring choices of Charles and Dodi say something about each man, and each mans relationship with Diana. Maybe Charles never really knew her well enough. Or maybe Dodi doesn't. I've never really seen Diana wear that much jewellery before, except for important events with Charles. Other than that it seems to be small, delicate pieces that compliment her outfit, like pearls. Maybe that's all part of being the person she's expected to be though, conforming to the image she's expected to present. Maybe this marriage will see Diana blossom into the person she has always wanted to be, the person that she really is. A good relationship with the right person can do that to a girl.

CHAPTER SEVEN

Diana waits outside the plain wooden door, listening to the sounds of the meeting wrapping up. It has already overrun by fifteen minutes and she had arrived five minutes early. The long white corridor she is standing in offers little entertainment and nowhere for her to sit and rest her feet while she waits. Finally the solid brass globe begins to turn slowly and the door pushes open with a squeak. Several well dressed men begin to make their way out, talking amiably, shaking hands and saying goodbye. Upon catching sight of Diana the men falter and conversation stutters to nothing. Clearly unsure of how to behave in front of her, the men mumble their greetings before disappearing off, leaving only Dodi behind. Smiling broadly he takes Diana gently into his arms and kisses her softly

"You mentioned that your meeting would end at around this time, I thought we could have some lunch together?"

Before Dodi can reply another voice calls out from inside the meeting room

"Is that my future daughter in law I can hear out in the hall?"

Blushing, Diana steps into the room and into the waiting embrace of Mohamed Al Fayed, his heavy arms surrounding her slender frame. Stepping back and kissing both her cheeks, he admires her momentarily before speaking

"Shall we get lunch, the three of us?"

Staring out across the dark restaurant, Mohamed Al Fayed chatters away happily about the couples plans for the wedding and the future. Seated as far away from the exit as possible, Diana and Dodi shift uncomfortably in the well padded chairs, their backs turned out toward the rest of the room.

"You're both still at a good age for producing children, I should like to see a grandson or a granddaughter arrive shortly after the wedding."

The gleam in Mohamed's eye suggested he was teasing, but his light hearted attempt to rib the couple was lost on both of them as they stare blankly back at him. The waiter arrives conveniently at the table, bearing three plates of food and breaking the awkward silence. Snapping out of her reverie slightly, Diana looks up at the waiter and smiles before saying

"Thank you, it looks lovely."

Despite the fact that she has not even looked at her food. Dodi and his father nod once at the waiter, who takes his leave and the three of them begin tucking into their meals. Picking up her knife, Diana cuts miniscule portions of meat from her plate and places them into her mouth before chewing them excessively. After each mouthful she picks up her napkin and dabs at her mouth gently. On the third occasion Diana makes an obvious pretence of dropping her napkin. She leans gracefully over the edge of her chair to retrieve it, simultaneously looking over her shoulder at the rest of the diners and the bustle of activity in the restaurant. Satisfied, she returns to an upright position and begins to chip away at her food once more, paying no attention to the two men she is dining with, both of whom are staring at her intently. It is Dodi who resumes eating first, leaving his father still staring at Diana before he also picks up a fork and continues with both his meal and the conversation.

"Have you given any thoughts to a possible date for the wedding?"

Diana doesn't look up at Mohammed as she replies

"It's not something that we've talked about yet. I'm sure we'll sit down soon and make some plans."

Dodi looks to his father and nods his agreement, before his eyes begin to wander around the room. In his lap, one hand worries against the corner of his napkin, the other concentrating on his food. Across the room a man laughs, a loud booming noise that fills the air. He gestures wildly, his glass slipping from his hand, the smash echoing off of the cold marble floor. Both Diana and Dodi jump visibly, their heads snapping up and their eyes searching for each other. The restaurant quietens momentarily, before normal chatter starts to resume and the waiters begin to clear up the mess of broken glass. Still staring at each other, it takes Diana and Dodi several moments before they seem to remember that they are not alone. Dodi breathes deeply before forcing a soft laugh and attempting to make light of the situation.

"Someone has clearly had a bit too much to drink."

He picks up his wine glass and takes a small sip to reiterate his point and Diana follows suit. Across the

table Mohammed studies the pair intently, his d
boring into them.

"What's going on?"

His tone is serious, filled with concern. It is Diana who
answers, her voice carefully light and full of surprise

"I don't know what you mean."

"You're like a pair of frightened rabbits, barely
speaking, eyes darting all over the place as if you're
watching out for predators. You practically leapt out of
your seats all for a bit of broken glass. Has something
happened? Is someone threatening you?"

Both Diana and Dodi open their mouths to reassure
him, but he carries on

"Both of you have increased the amount of protection
you have around you. I didn't say anything because
I thought it was a wise move, you can never be too
careful. But why now? Is it something to do with the
engagement? Have you been threatened?"

Diana looks to Dodi, her face pleading with him to calm
his father down.

"Dad, nothing is wrong. We've increased security
because, like you, we thought it would be a smart move.
There have been no threats, no issues, nothing at all to
worry about. Now, have you had any ideas about where
we could hold the wedding?"

Disbelief fills Mohammed's eyes, but, grateful for a
chance to talk about the wedding, he accepts the subject
change. Over dessert and coffee the trio chatter lightly
about the trivialities of the wedding, a warm smile

growing across father and sons faces as they talk about welcoming Diana into their family. Diana joins in the conversation as much as she can, her eyes still keenly sweeping the room, her hands tightly clamped between her legs.

The trio exchange warm hugs in farewell as the sky darkens to early evening. Talk of the wedding had stretched right through the afternoon, endless cups of coffee being delivered to the table. Diana had made a good effort to stay involved, or at least keep up, with the conversation, but several times she had got lost in her own thoughts only to come round and find Dodi or his father staring at her in silent concern. It had been Dodi who suggested they spend the night somewhere local and Diana had readily agreed. Several phone calls later, Diana and Dodi had both cleared their schedules for the following day and were awaiting a car to take them to the Savoy.

"I think we should travel separately."

Dodi stares at Diana, her head bowed to the floor as she speaks.

"Excuse me?"

Keeping her head low and staring intently at the menu as if she hadn't been sitting in the restaurant all afternoon, Diana repeats herself

"I think we should travel to the hotel separately. Check into separate rooms even. Or you could arrive and check in and maybe someone could let me in through the back? I don't really want to stay here by myself though, so maybe I should go first? Someone might see me checking in though, so maybe you should go first."

Diana raises her head briefly and is greeted by Dodi staring at her intently.

"Are you seriously suggesting one of us should creep into the Savoy through a back entrance like some adulterous couple?"

His voice is filled with incredulity. Diana stares back at him, her blue eyes icy cold, and doesn't answer. He tries reasoning with her again

"Diana, we're getting married. People are going to expect to see us out and about together, the press are going to want to take photos of us as a couple...."

His voice trails off as she lowers her head and begins studying the menu intently once more. After a few moments he sighs and gets wearily to his feet

"I'll call for another car."

Diana had stopped the car twice on the way to the hotel and had barely made it there before Dodi. Wrapping her coat around her, Diana enters the foyer of the hotel wearing large dark sunglasses, a wide straw hat covering her distinctive hair. Speaking in hushed tones to the concierge, she advises him that she will be spending the night and expects her privacy to be protected at all costs. Taking her key and making the way towards the lift, Diana sends one member of her security team to go and find Dodi, whilst another waits with her for the lift to arrive. A young, well dressed couple smile warmly at Diana as they also wait for the lift. Ignoring them, she turns her head and addresses her bodyguard in muted tones, before looking back to the floor as he quietly informs the couple that it would be in their best interest to take the stairs.

The room is beautiful, tastefully decorated with breathtaking views. Diana had met Dodi in the hallway and the pair had been escorted to their rooms, careful not to be seen. It was only once the door was safely closed on the couple that Diana felt comfortable enough to remove her disguise. Located discreetly up and down the corridor several armed bodyguards keep watch, instructed by Diana to not let anyone near to their room. As Dodi holds his arms out to embrace Diana she slides from his grasp and begins examining the room, paying particular attention to the windows and door. Once she is satisfied with these she sits down on the bed and picks up the telephone, listening to the dial tone before leaving the handset off the hook and placing it on the table. She stares at the receiver for a moment before picking it up and placing it back in the cradle. Still not satisfied, Diana once again goes to remove the phone from off the hook.

"Diana, this is ridiculous. No one knows we are here. We didn't know we were coming here."

Dodi's brown eyes plead with her as she stands up and once again begins walking around the room.

"Please, just relax. We're perfectly safe here, we've taken enough precautions. Let's just enjoy some time alone."

Diana stares at him for what seems an eternity before smiling softly

"I'm being silly, aren't I?"

Dodi smiles back at her, reaching forward to take both her hands in his

"It's understandable that you're frightened. We had quite a scare and I think it's made us both a little paranoid. I think it would be best for both of us if we just tried to put that night behind us and get on with our lives. It was an unfortunate accident and we were incredibly lucky. Let's just be grateful for that."

He pulls Diana towards him and envelopes her in his arms, kissing the top of her head softly. She closes her eyes, seeming to lose herself in his embrace momentarily, before breaking free at a hurried pace. Dashing to the bathroom, she lets the door slam loudly behind her before the sounds of her retching echo off of the tiled walls, floating back into the room where Dodi is waiting.

CHAPTER EIGHT

Diana stares down forlornly at the little white plastic stick in her hand. Several other used pregnancy tests litter the floor around her, all showing the same thing. Positive. Crossing her legs, Diana leans back against the cold porcelain of the toilet and examines the test with an unreadable look on her face. Sighing, she drops the test to the floor and leans forward again to place her head into her delicate white hands. Breathing deeply she closes her eyes, muttering to herself.

"What does this mean? What am I going to do? What happens now?"

Over and over she repeats the refrain, as if somehow all the answers will come to her. Suddenly her head snaps up, her blue eyes wide with fear. Bending low, she gathers up all of the used pregnancy tests and leaps off of the toilet. The bathroom door swings wildly behind her as she dashes into her bedroom and frantically stuffs the tests into her handbag, doing up the clasp tightly. Diana frantically sweeps the bedroom, pulling the curtains closed and checking that the door is locked. She collapses on the bed once her checks are complete, breathing quickly and covering her face with her hands. Her bag falls from the bed as she lays down, the clasp flicks open with the tests once again spilling on to the floor. Tears flow freely down Diana's cheeks as she moves slowly to the floor to gather them up once more.

Dodi stares at Diana, seated on the floor across from him as he relaxes on the expensive sofa. Her bare feet tucked underneath her, she looks vulnerable, her skin even paler than usual. A fire burns softly in the corner of the room, illuminating the touches of gold littered amongst the cream decor. She had spent almost fifteen minutes checking the room thoroughly when they had arrived, looking under every cushion and in every plant pot. When Dodi had asked what she was looking for she had been unable to tell him, explaining only that she had to be certain it was safe before they spoke. Clearly unwilling to push her, he had watched her with a bemused smile on his face, relaxing only when she lowered herself elegantly onto the plush carpet, her back leaning against the coffee table.

"I'm pregnant."

The words came out of her mouth in a rush, as if she were desperate to be rid of them. Once she has spoken Diana stares at the carpet, picking intently at a loose weave while she waits for Dodi's response.

"That's fantastic!"

Dodi's voice is filled with enthusiasm, he moves excitedly out of his seat, making as if to embrace Diana. Her cold stare stops him dead in his tracks.

"What's the matter? Aren't you pleased?"

Genuine concern and confusion spread across Dodi's face as he stares at Diana, her face still carefully blank.

"I don't know!"

She finally answers

"Am I supposed to be?"

Her voice is quiet but firm, her eyes icy as she stares at Dodi.

"What's that supposed to mean?"

"It means a million things. It means we never even discussed having children. It means is it the best time to be bringing a child into the world? It means isn't it frowned upon for us to have sex when we're not married? It means what are we going to do?"

Dodi stares at Diana for a moment, letting her regain her cool once she has said all she needed to. When he answers her his tone is soothing, pacifying.

"It means we're having a baby. Of course it does. Would you really even consider not having it?"

Diana considers for a moment before shaking her head softly as Dodi continues.

"A baby is a blessing, regardless of whether the timing is right. If people only had babies when the timing was perfect then there would be no children in the world. There is always going to be a reason why it isn't the perfect time, but if we love each other enough to have made a baby together then we have an obligation to give that baby the life he or she deserves."

Dodi's tone softens even further as he coos to Diana

"I know you'd love a baby girl."

Diana smiles shyly for a moment, before concern once again spreads across her face

"What about your religion? Isn't sex before marriage seen as a terrible sin?"

Dodi considers for a moment before replying carefully.

"I must ask for forgiveness. You should too, I imagine Christianity is not much different in that respect. The baby will be raised a Muslim, of course. Perhaps for your sake we should also hurry the wedding along, legitimise the baby as soon as possible. That would probably be better for your public image too, not being seen as a fornicator."

Dodi is practically musing to himself, almost as if he has forgotten that Diana is in the room. She rises to her feet slowly, positioning herself in front of him so he is forced to look at her.

"Don't I get a say in any of this? Don't I get to pick what religion my child will be? When my wedding will be? Next you'll be picking out my dress and telling me what the baby's name is."

Her voice shakes with anger and defiance as she stares Dodi down, interrupting his monologue. Before he has a chance to respond she storms from the room, letting the heavy oak door slam behind her and leaving Dodi standing alone in front of the fire.

"Diana's pregnant."

Dodi watches as a look of glee spreads across his fathers face.

"That explains why you two were so edgy the other day. That is fantastic news!"

Mohammad Al Fayed embraces his son warmly before pulling away and examining his face.

"You are not pleased?"

Dodi runs his hands through his hair before holding them in front of him, palms turned towards the sky.

"It's not that I'm not pleased, a baby is a blessing. It's Diana."

The elder Al Fayed looks puzzled.

"I would have thought she would be pleased to have more children?"

Dodi leans forward as if inviting his father into his confidence

"I don't think that she isn't pleased to be having another child, more that it's so unexpected. She's being...."

Dodi's voice trails off, only resuming speaking when his father prompts him.

"Difficult."

He sighs deeply, his hands returning to his head to gently massage his temples. His father waits patiently for him to continue, their silence seeming to fill the room. Eventually Dodi speaks

"She won't talk about setting a date for the wedding. I wanted to do something quickly. Legitimise the baby before it is even born. Get us started as a family."

Mohammed thinks for a few moments before replying to his son.

"Of course, marrying as soon as possible would be the best idea, but it is a new world we live in Dodi, things are not the same as they were. Diana has agreed to marry you, I think that is the important thing. Of course, the Holy Qur'an does teach of the evils of fornication outside of marriage, but I do not think in this day people will look too harshly on you if you are clearly intending to wed. Plus, the child will of course be raised in the Muslim faith, so you will be doing the best by your family."

Dodi clears his throat uncomfortably. When he speaks his voice is meek.

"Diana refuses to discuss the child's religion. She says she will not be dictated to."

Mohammad chuckles softly to himself.

"You got yourself involved with a strong woman, this is the cross you have to bear. Diana is sensible though, educate her. Show her what Islam has to offer a child. I believe she will make the right decision."

"And if she doesn't? More to the point, if she does? Diana and I never discussed having children, but she's a very popular woman. I don't know how people might react to her having a Muslim child. Not everyone is as open minded as she is. Most people are ignorant, unable or unwilling to see the beauty of Islam, or even its similarities to Christianity."

Dodi paces in a circle around his father, dry washing his hands as he speaks.

"Son, you need to relax. Yes, I agree, Diana is an incredibly popular woman, so this can only mean good things for Islam. If she shows her openness to our religion it may mean that others will be more willing to do the same. If Diana herself were to convert it would be even better. She could bring Islam into mainstream Britain. Spreading the word of Allah is a noble thing to do. I know you are concerned about the reactions within our community, but I think most people will realise that by raising the profile of Islam you are doing Allah and the Prophet Mohammad, peace be upon him, great service."

Dodi considers his father's words for a moment before reaching into his jacket and removing an envelope from his inside pocket and flinging it down onto his father's desk. The old man looks up at his son before reaching down to the envelope and sliding a folded piece of paper out from within. Printed on heavy paper, in large letters taking up most of the page

"*As for the fornicatress, none shall marry her but a fornicator or an idolater, and it is forbidden to believers.*"

Mohammad breathes deeply before folding the paper and placing it back inside the envelope.

"I can understand that this is worrying Dodi, but it is nothing but the work of an interfering busybody. You cannot please all of the people all of the time."

Dodi picks up the envelope and places it back in his inside pocket.

"I wouldn't normally be worried, except that it was hand delivered, through my front door in the middle of the night. None of my security team saw or heard anything."

The two men study each other intently, both of them appearing deeply concerned.

"Did you tell the police?"

Dodi's voice sounds tired as he responds.

"What's the point? It's not as if it's even a threat really, just a reminder of something someone thinks I should know. Even if it was a threat the police wouldn't do anything about it. Look at how helpful they were in Paris."

Mohammad looks at his son.

"Why would the police have needed to help with a car accident?"

Dodi looks up at his father, his dark eyes troubled.

"Nothing, no, I didn't mean help, I just meant be there."

Mohammad's eyebrows furrow together

"The police were there. You and Diana disappeared, it took us hours to find you."

Dodi shrugs his shoulders, murmuring his agreement before continuing on his pacing of the room.

"I'm getting anonymous letters because I'm intending to marry Diana, what's going to happen when people find out that she's pregnant?"

"Son, I think you're forgetting about the millions of people who are happy about your union. People who are pleased that both of you have found happiness with each other. Don't let one little letter detract from that."

Sighing deeply, Dodi responds

"I suppose you're right. I'm sure this will be a one off."

"If I may offer a little advice?"

Dodi smiles at his father, encouraging his confidence.

"It is not wise to let a woman stew in her own juices. Talk to Diana, let her explain her worries and fears. Put your points across. You are both grownups, perhaps now is the time to start behaving as such."

Dodi smiles at his father, reaching forward to clasp both his hands within his own.

"Those are the words of a truly wise man. I will speak to Diana."

Releasing his father's hands, Dodi makes his way towards the door, he stops as Mohammad calls to him.

"I wouldn't tell Diana about the letter. It will only worry her unnecessarily."

Dodi's face clouds with concern momentarily, before smiling warmly at his father and making his way out of the door.

CHAPTER NINE

Diana winces slightly as the cold jelly is applied to her stomach and clutches Dodi's hand. She had insisted, once again, that they arrive separately to the doctor's office. Dodi hadn't bothered to argue this time, simply booking himself another car and smiling patiently at Diana. When he had arrived at the expensive, Harley Street surgery, his driver had taken him to a small side entrance away from any photographers who might be laying in wait. Once inside he had been directed straight into the doctors office by a nurse who had been instructed to wait for his arrival. Diana had been seated in front of the smiling doctor, carefully removing a long dark wig and placing it on the floor next to her handbag, an oversized pair of sunglasses and a large black hat. She smiled serenely at Dodi and motioned for him to sit next to her.

The sonographer moves the plastic wand in circles over Diana's still flat stomach until a grainy image appears on the monitor next to him. The faint thump of a heartbeat echoes from the speakers and the outline of a foetus comes in and out of focus with each wave of the wand. Diana props herself up on her elbows and stares at the screen, taking in the tiny form of the child growing inside her. The doctors voice breaks through her reverie.

"Everything looks perfectly healthy, you look to be about eight weeks a long. It's too early to tell if you are expecting a boy or a girl, but they will be able to tell you at your twenty week scan should you want to know."

The Doctor smiles warmly at Diana and Dodi, and presses a few buttons on the keyboard beneath the monitor. A few seconds later a fuzzy black and white image prints out from the machine. Smiling, the doctor hands it over to Diana before excusing himself to give the couple a few moments alone.

"Eight weeks......"

Dodi lets the statement hang in the air while they both consider the implications of his words. It is Diana who breaks the silence.

"Well it was hardly likely to have been after Paris, we haven't been near each other."

Her voice is cold and detached as she reaches for a tissue and begins to wipe the jelly from her stomach.

"I actually meant that the baby went through the accident the same as we did and he or she has survived. Eight weeks is supposed to be the safe point too, isn't it? The point when it's OK to start telling people that you're expecting? Maybe we can check that with the doctor."

Diana's head snaps up and her gaze fixes intently on Dodi.

"Telling people now?"

Dodi stares at her for a moment as if trying to gauge her mood.

"Well, we're going to have to tell people at some point and you'll probably start showing soon."

Diana's eyes flash with temper

"Are you trying to imply that I look overweight? You want to tell the world that I'm pregnant so people don't just presume you're marrying a whale?"

"Come on Diana, be reasonable. Of course I don't think that. However, you are pregnant so at some point you are going to put weight on. Wouldn't it be better that the story came from us rather than having the press hound you even more than they already are? Filling the newspapers with speculative stories?"

Diana sighs deeply, her shoulders dropping as if in defeat.

"I suppose you're right, although could we hold off for a little while longer? Please?"

Dodi shrugs his shoulders in agreement, before taking the tissue that Diana holds out to him and dropping it in the bin. She rearranges her clothes so that she is once again fully covered up and swings her legs over the side of the bed. Taking the hand that Dodi offers, she drops gracefully onto the balls of her feet and straightens up to her full height. Dropping his hand, Diana marches ahead of Dodi back into the doctor's office.

Diana checks and rechecks her reflection several times before she steps out of the back entrance of the clinic. Her blonde hair tucked away once more under the dark wig and hat and half of her face covered by the sunglasses, she practically blends into the shadows that are creeping up the alley. Waiting at the end of the lane is her black four by four, engine running, and several dark suited men waiting to escort Diana home. Dodi, once again made to travel by himself despite their destination being the same, kisses her chastely on the cheek before walking to the opposite end of the alley to wait for his Mercedes to arrive. Without looking over her shoulder, Diana steps into her vehicle, strapping herself firmly into place and gripping tightly onto the edge of her seat. She remains in silence for the entire journey, forsaking her usual refrains of please and thank you to her driver and security team. Several tears drizzle out from beneath her sunglasses, dropping onto the black heavy wool coat that completes her disguise and remaining there as if they are frozen. Diana does not move her hands from their position to check the flow or wipe down her coat, instead remaining fixed to the spot. Lightning flashes across the sky, briefly illuminating the throng of traffic still clogging up the London streets. Diana jumps, a small scream escaping from her lips at the following crash of thunder. Her breathing turns ragged as her head twists from window to window as if looking for the source of the light and noise. She pays no attention to the driver staring in concern at her through the rear view mirror and tightens her grip on the seat beneath her. As the second bolt of lightning flashes across the sky, Diana inhales loud enough to be heard across the hum of the engine and vomits across the floor in front of her just as the second rumble of thunder begins.

Diana awakes in a pale blue room, the flimsy cloth curtains pulled across the window doing nothing to stop the cold autumn sunlight from streaming in. She moves slowly, pulling the layers of sheets and blankets off of herself with difficulty and slowly positioning her legs at the side of the bed. Two unfamiliar slippers wait there and she slips her feet inside them. Diana raises herself to a standing position with difficulty, using the pale wooden bedside cabinet to steady herself as she wobbles slightly. She shuffles towards the window, her bag positioned on a functional plastic chair beneath it, but before she can make it the door opens and an elderly nurse bustles in.

"Ooh you shouldn't be out of bed until the doctor has seen you. How are you feeling my love?"

The nurse hurries on without waiting for a reply

"You gave everyone quite a scare, passing out like that. Good job your driver had the sense to bring you straight to the hospital. Now love, what would you like for breakfast?"

Diana ignores the question

"I passed out? In the car?"

The nurse nods her confirmation, still holding a pen and paper and waiting for a response to her earlier question.

"Who knows I'm here?"

Diana spits out the question and the nurse visibly flinches at the tone of her voice. When she responds it is meek, trembling slightly.

"Well, your fiancé of course. He was here last night, although the doctor told him you needed to rest and sent him home. I believe Princes William and Harry have also been informed Ma'am."

The nurse looks to the floor and shuffles her feet uncomfortably as if unsure if she has said the right thing.

"Press?"

This time Diana's voice is weak, almost frightened. When the nurse looks up again she finds herself staring into Diana's blue eyes, wide with panic.

"No Ma'am. A couple of newspapers have called saying they had a tip off you were here, a couple of journalists turned up too, but we managed to convince them that they'd been given bad information."

There is a hint of pride in the nurses voice, as if she personally had something to do with hoodwinking the media. Diana's posture relaxes at the news and she makes her way slowly back to the bed and sits down gracefully.

"Thank you. I think I'd like some toast, wholemeal please. And some orange juice."

The nurse scribbles hurriedly onto her paper and smiles widely at Diana

"The doctor will be in to see you once you have eaten."

And closes the door softly behind her as she leaves the room. Left to herself, Diana examines the cotton robe, pulling gently at a lose thread. The sound of a trolley being wheeled up the corridor makes her flinch and the slam of another patients door startles her. By the time the nurse arrives with her toast, Diana is sitting cross legged in the middle of the bed, pale as a sheet, her hands gripping the covers as if she is afraid she might fall off. She does not look at the nurse, simply taking the plate and glass as they are offered to her and waiting in silence for the woman to leave. When the doctor arrives, not five minutes later, Diana is still holding the glass and the plate, staring intently at the floor.

"Diana?"

She does not look up at the sound of her name, remaining locked in the same position until the doctor puts a comforting hand on her shoulder.

"How are you feeling?"

Diana smiles weakly in response, her hands starting to shake and orange juice sloshing onto the covers.

"You were examined when you were admitted last night, the first thing we did once we were aware of your condition was check the baby's heartbeat."

Diana's eyes dart to the closed door and the window as soon as the baby is mentioned, before resting on the doctor and examining him intently.

"The baby is fine. It isn't uncommon for expectant mothers to pass out, especially when they are as early on as you are. We would like to do an ultrasound just to make sure, but I think what you really need is some rest. Time to put your feet up and relax, being pregnant is hard work."

The doctor smiles a wide grin that does its best to reach his tired eyes and begins to make his way towards the door.

"I'm going to send someone in to take you down to have your scan, but providing that is all fine you'll be able to go home soon."

He opens the door and begins to make his way when Diana calls him back, her voice hoarse and low

"The press, no one knows, that I'm here, that I'm......"

She does not finish the sentence, waiting for the doctor to fill in the blanks.

"Pregnant? I can assure you that no one here would say a word to anyone about a patient, but because of your status we have made sure that only a very small team of doctors and nurses have been dealing with you. Everyone is on a need to know basis, and those that need to know would not say a word."

He smiles warmly once more at Diana, who manages a small smile in response, before leaving. As he is making his way out of the door, the doctor almost collides with Dodi who is on his way in. Both men mutter their apologies before carrying on their respective ways. Dodi, his arms laden with flowers, makes his way to Diana's bed. He leans forward to kiss her, struggling under the weight of the blooms in his arms. Diana turns her head so that Dodi's kiss lands on her cheek and motions to the table for him to place the flowers there. As he begins to question her on her health, Diana cuts him off with a question of her own

"Did you come in the back way? Did anyone see you? Where did you get the flowers from? Were you seen buying them?"

Dodi looks confused by all the questions, but before he can respond she begins again

"What phone did you use to tell the boys I was here? What driver did you use to bring you here? Are you sure there were no press following you? You really shouldn't have come."

Her voice is heavy as if the world is conspiring against her, her shoulders sagging. Dodi looks hurt at Diana's last statement and opens his mouth to respond, but before he can speak there is a knock at the door and the elderly nurse who had brought Diana breakfast enters.

"Now, my love, Dr Richards said we were to take you down to have a scan."

Diana begins to move slowly off of the bed

"No no dear, don't you move yourself about, we'll wheel you down there. Don't you worry yourself."

Diana sinks back down on to the bed and watches with empty eyes as the nurse begins securing the sides of the bed and taking the brakes off of the wheels.

"You're having a scan? Is everything OK? The baby?"

Dodi's voice is panicked, his eyes stretched wide. Diana doesn't answer, leaving the questions hanging in the air. Finally, the nurse responds, her voice soothing

"It's nothing to worry about love, just a precaution. You'll more than likely be taking her home to rest this afternoon."

Dodi smiles warmly and holds the door open as the nurse begins to push the bed out into the corridor and towards the lifts. As the trio turn the corner they are greeted by a horde of photographers, hiding out of sight. They smile greedily at their prize, raising their cameras hurriedly and immortalising forever Diana's horrified expression.

CHAPTER TEN

Diana stares forlornly at her horrified image gazing up from the front page of the newspaper. Her hair was matted and unkempt, her pale skin practically blending in with the vanilla colour scheme of the hospital walls. Dodi's face was angry, his dark features twisted towards the camera and his arm reaching out in an effort to stop the photo being taken. Clearly he had been unsuccessful, although it had only been the one photo that was taken before the photographers had scarpered. That one horrible photo had graced the front page of every single newspaper across the country. Millions of people had woken up to find Diana, frozen in horror on a hospital gurney, waiting for them on their doormat. The headlines screamed about Diana's mystery illness, speculating about what could be wrong with her, although they all seemed to be aware that she had collapsed in the car. Diana threw down the paper in frustration.

"Someone told them I was here."

Diana speaks aloud to herself. Although the scan had showed that the baby was perfectly healthy, the doctors and nurses had decided to keep her in overnight, just for further observation. She had been reluctant, wanting to get home now the press knew for sure where she was, but the doctor had insisted. She had stayed awake all night, covers pulled up to her chin, staring at the ceiling and starting at every noise until she had eventually fallen asleep in the early hours. Exhausted, a few tears had slipped from her eyes when she had been greeted with her own image staring back at her from the newspaper brought in with breakfast. Toast and orange juice lay untouched in her lap as she mutters to herself.

"The doctor said no one here would have said anything, that hardly anyone knew. But that was about being pregnant. Lots of people know I'm here. The lady that emptied the bin could have called them. Or the man that cleaned the floor. It could have been the doctor, or one of the nurses. But then you'd think they would have said about the baby. Dodi could have mentioned it to someone. It could have been his driver. It could have been my driver. Maybe someone is listening to his phone. Maybe someone is listening in on the boys phone. Maybe it was a lucky guess."

Diana laughs a high pitched laugh to herself, stopping as the door opens tentatively. Hurriedly she opens the newspaper and pretends to be engrossed in an article as the nurse comes in to remove her breakfast things. She tuts softly when she sees the still full plate and glass.

"You really should eat something love, if not for your sake then for the baby."

Diana does not look up as the nurse speaks to her.

"Plus if you don't eat or drink, you'll only pass out again and end up right back in here."

Diana looks up into the nurses face and reaches out to take back the glass of orange juice. The nurse smiles as she takes a sip.

71

"That's it love. Now, the doctor will be in to see you soon and I would think you'll be going home not long after."

Diana smiles weakly, before taking another sip of juice and watching the nurse leave.

Dodi turns up just as the doctor is leaving, the two men chat briefly in the doorway before Dodi turns to Diana.

"The doctor says it's OK for me to take you home, as long as you take it easy for a few days."

A broad smile stretches across his face

"Isn't that great news?"

Diana's returning smile is thin and false. She holds out a piece of paper to Dodi.

"I'll be needing these before I leave. And we'll have to talk about what we're going to say to the press about why I was in here."

Dodi opens his mouth to say something, but Diana cuts him off

"I'm not ready to tell people if that's what you're about to say. The newspapers all know I collapsed so we're going to have to be really careful what we say in front of anyone. It will probably be best to say it was exhaustion or dehydration. That way people won't question why I need to rest and take things easy for a bit."

She does not look at Dodi the whole time she is speaking, instead staring intently at her own image on the newspaper still strewn across the bed. Dodi looks down to the list Diana has given him and begins to read out loud

"Clean clothes, toiletries, make up........"

His voice trails off as his eyes scan the rest of the list

"Is the disguise really necessary? Everyone already knows you're here."

Diana stares at him coldly

"There is no reason for them to know any more though is there? I don't want to be harassed by photographers on my way home."

"So, I take it we'll also be travelling separately again then? Otherwise the newspapers will be full of stories of me out with a mystery brunette while you were laid up in the hospital."

Diana ignores the laughter in Dodi's voice and simply nods to answer his question. Dodi sighs and begins examining the list once more..

"Sanitary towels?"

He stares at Diana in confusion.

"Well I presumed you were going to get one of the staff to pack my bag, if they think I need them then they won't guess that I'm pregnant and won't be able to call the press."

Her voice is calm and even, the faintest hint of mockery in her tone.

"Don't you think you're blowing this out of proportion a bit? Anyone could have told the press you were here, any of the doctors or nurses, another patient, someone visiting. Your staff have been with you a long time, I thought you trusted them?"

Diana hangs her head as she replies in a low tone
"So did I."
Diana waits alone in her room for Dodi to arrive. When she had arrived at home her staff had been both surprised and pleased to see her, with many offering their get well wishes. Diana had smiled a tight lipped smile and thanked them, before heading straight up to her room. Dodi didn't bother to knock, instead letting himself straight into the room and wrapping Diana into his arms. The pair hold their embrace for a while, before breaking away. Dodi seems shocked to find tears rolling down Diana's face. Cupping her chin gently he looks into her eyes, concern written all over his face
"What's wrong?"

Diana takes a deep breath before dissolving into complete hysterics. Dodi makes his way into the bathroom, remerging several seconds later with a wad of tissue and a glass of water. He guides Diana to the bed and helps her to sit before handing her the tissue and the drink. After taking several deep gulps of water and blowing her nose, she finally manages to speak
"We're having a baby."

Dodi's face crumples up in confusion to her comment. He doesn't speak, but waits for her to continue.
"Someone tried to kill us......"

Diana's voice trails off and neither of them speak. Several full minutes pass before Dodi has gathered his thoughts enough to respond. His voice is low, his expression tired.

"We don't know that."

Diana looks at him, temper flashing in her eyes.

"I think we both knew it was deliberate that night. Why else would you have been so keen for us to get away from the crash? If it was an accident we could have just waited around for help. You wanted to make sure we weren't sitting around for someone to come back and finish the job."

Diana's voice is quiet but there is steel behind her words. All trace of tears are gone from her eyes, although their remnants still mark her face. Dodi doesn't respond, instead looking to the floor to avoid her penetrative gaze.

"What if they try again?"

Diana's voice is softer, filled with worry. Dodi raises his gaze to meet hers as she continues.

"It's not just us to worry about now, and I don't know who I can trust or what I should do. What if they try again and we're not so lucky? What if they try again when I'm with William and Harry, picking them up from school or taking them out for the day? I don't feel safe, I don't know who, if anyone, I can talk to, where, if anywhere, is safe for me to be."

Diana's voice softens to almost a whisper as she looks to Dodi and admits

"I'm scared."

Dodi wraps Diana in his arms, holding her petite frame against his chest and strokes her hair. Tears begin to fall from her eyes again, sobs hiccoughing through her body. Dodi presses kisses into her hair, stopping at her temple and muttering hoarsely into her ear

"I am too."

He places his hand behind Diana's head and pulls her even closer to him, before relaxing into a laying position. Diana places one hand over his heart and puts her head tentatively on his chest, listening to the regular thump of his heart beating. The occasional tear slips from her eyes, making damp patches on Dodi's heavy white shirt. He continues to run his fingers through her hair, murmuring soft words of reassurance that Diana does not appear to hear. After about ten minutes like this, Diana rolls to her right, settling on her back in the middle of the bed and looking up at the ceiling.

"Am I starting to show yet?"

Dodi eyes his fiancés perfectly flat stomach with suspicion, as if unsure there is a right answer to her question.

"Not yet, no."

Diana props herself up onto her elbows and looks him in the eye

"I will start so show fairly soon though, if my last two pregnancies are anything to go by. Plus I'm older now, so I'll probably get even bigger. You were right earlier, I'd rather tell the press than have them speculating. Or, finding out some other way."

Diana looks at Dodi as a huge smile spreads across his face. He reaches out and places one of his large hands tentatively on top of her stomach. Diana looks down and laughs softly as he spreads his fingers to reach across the whole width of her torso.

"You won't be able to do that for much longer."

Dodi laughs and agrees
"Not with my strapping boy in there."

Diana pretends to be outraged
"What makes you think we're having a boy? I think there is a beautiful little ballerina in there."

They grin at each other, the charade broken. Dodi leaves his hand on Diana's stomach and begins to rub gently in tiny circles
"We haven't talked about names yet."

All traces of laughter gone from her smile, Diana considers the question before responding with one of her own.
"Do you really think we're having a boy? Whenever I try to picture having the baby I always imagine a girl, and she's always a little blue eyed blonde. I suppose that's not very likely is it?"

Dodi smiles softly
"I really don't know what we're having, I really don't care. All that matters is that you're healthy and the baby is healthy. But you're right, I don't think a little blue eyed blonde is very likely."

He chuckles softly to himself.
"What about names?"

The question comes up again and Diana considers for a moment before responding.

"What about Isabella for a girl?"

Dodi's face wrinkles up as if in disgust and Diana laughs
"I take it that's a no then! What we're you thinking?"
"What about Madiha? Or Ameera?"

Diana mimics the face that Dodi made at her suggestion and they both laugh.
"I suppose we still have plenty of time to think about it."

Dodi smiles at Diana, leaning up to kiss her lips softly. They pull apart quickly at the sound of the door clicking shut, hurriedly sitting up and staring at the now closed doorway. Dodi pushes himself off of the bed and hurries towards the entrance, flinging the door wide open and staring out into the empty corridor. He takes a few steps into the hall, first looking to his right and then to his left. Seeing no one, he returns to the room and shrugs his shoulders at Diana, still sitting on the bed. Pulling her knees up to her chin, she wraps her arms around them as if she is trying to hold herself together. Breathing deeply, she asks
"I wonder how long they were there. What they saw. How much they heard."

Dodi makes his way towards the bed, perching on the end with his back to Diana. Neither of them speak for several moments, before Diana concedes in a small voice
"I suppose we had better speak to the PR team, call a press conference. Before someone else does."

CHAPTER ELEVEN

God this lecture is dragging. It's only been twenty minutes but it already feels like hours. I've doodled in all the margins of the paper I'm supposed to be making notes on and gossiped about the latest news with the girl sitting next to me. Couldn't tell you her name, but she seems to pay attention about as much as I do in these things. Honestly, I'd thought about blowing the lecture off, but I've been doing a lot of that recently. There is something about early nineteenth century literature that bores me to tears. Plus the cold auditorium and the uncomfortable seats don't help. I'd much rather have stayed home and caught the rest of the press conference in my pyjamas. I couldn't believe it when I switched on, after another helpful phone call from my mother. I swear all that woman does is spend her life glued to the TV. Still, I'm glad she did.

My first thought when I turned the TV on was that Diana and Dodi were going to announce the date for their wedding. Good news, interesting, but not really worth the press conference. Still, it's always nice to have a peek at what Diana is wearing and how she's got her hair. But then they made the announcement and I was like wow. Oh my god. A baby. Well I didn't see that coming. I'd known Diana had been hospital this week after she collapsed but I thought it would just have been from stress or something like that. I never imagined she'd be pregnant. I wonder if she knew? Maybe she didn't find out until she was in the hospital. She said in the press conference that she was eight weeks gone so it's no wonder that she still looks so slim. Still, I guess that won't last long so that's probably why they're telling people now. Dodi looked so happy at the press conference, like all of his Christmases had come at once. Or whatever they have. It's hard to tell what people really mean sometimes, from the way things are so carefully worded. Diana and Dodi's statement was pretty standard actually, didn't really say anything different from what anyone else in the public eye would have said. They were pleased to announce that they were expecting blah blah blah. Answered a few questions, posed for photos with Dodi's hand on Diana's perfectly flat stomach. She didn't look too pleased about that if you ask me, but she smiled like she was supposed to.

A couple of the reporters asked Diana if she was hoping for a little girl this time round. Bog standard answer again; as long as the baby is healthy then they're happy. It would be nice though, after two boys. And if she was half as beautiful as her mother she'd be a gorgeous little girl. Although I suppose there isn't much chance either a boy or a girl looking like Diana, or their brothers either. No chance of another little porcelain blue eyed blonde. Not to say that he or she won't still be beautiful, just different is all. Take after their daddy. I wonder if they'll be rushing the wedding forward in light of the pregnancy? I grabbed a newspaper on the way to class and have been trying to read through it on the sly. All it said about the wedding was that a date had still not been confirmed, but I wouldn't be surprised if it was pushed forward a bit. Maybe they got engaged because they knew they were expecting a baby and just had to wait until now to tell people? It's certainly the expected thing to do, shotgun wedding and all that. But then you think they would have rushed the wedding and tried to pass the baby off as a honeymoon baby. Maybe they genuinely didn't know and when they found out wanted to tell the press before the media started speculating in a few months. It can't be nice to have people trying to guess what's going on in your life, or finding out things that you were trying to keep quiet. Much better to give out information on your own terms I suppose, try and prevent the constant invasion on your privacy. I mean, look at the photos of poor Diana in the hospital. She looked awful, and Dodi looked furious. Clearly they'd not expected to be confronted by photographers and who needs that when you're laid up in the hospital feeling rough? God, she must have been terrified that they'd find out she was pregnant then, that probably had something to do with the sudden press conference as well. I'd be livid if someone jumped out on me while I was in hospital, must be worse if you've got a secret you're trying to keep from the world.

I wonder if getting Diana pregnant has made Dodi a bit of an outcast. I thought it was a bit odd when they announced they were getting married; I didn't know it was ok to marry someone from a different religion, from either of their point of view. But more from the Muslim side really. They seem more strict, to have more iron clad rules than Christianity. They certainly don't seem as forgiving. Do something wrong as a Christian and you pretty much go to church and say you're sorry and it's all better. Somehow I don't think it works that way for Muslims. Sex before marriage is a pretty big no no in every religion as well, one of the big rules. But then Diana has been married before, so I wonder how that works. And what about the baby? What will he or she be? Diana brought William and Harry up as Christian, but that's because both her and Charles are Christian. How will it work with each parent having a different religion? Will they get a bit of both? Or maybe wait until they're a bit older and let them pick themselves? I wonder if either Diana or Dodi know the answers? Unless Diana is thinking of converting? She has turned over a pretty big new leaf recently. New life, new man. Maybe the final step is a brand new outlook on life. That would take away all the questions and potential problems that getting married and having a baby might cause. I never imagine a white woman when I think of a Muslim. In fact, I never really think of women at all. I always picture the older, Middle Eastern man with a long greying beard and wearing a robe that resembles a dress. I suppose that's like saying that all Christians wear tweed and thick round glasses. The stereotypical bible basher, I suppose there is one for every culture, every religion. It is hard to imagine Diana as a Muslim though. No more elegant clothes, nice make up and jewellery. She'd have to be almost completely covered all of the time, wouldn't she? I can't see her going for that, especially not with her charity work. People would never know that it was her. Although that could be a good thing when it comes to being hounded by the press I suppose. Aren't women inferior in most Middle Eastern cultures as well? Would that mean that Diana would have to be completely subservient to Dodi, all of the time? Because I really can't see her going for that either. Can you imagine Diana being constantly told how to look, speak and behave? That's part of what ruined her first marriage, I can't see her allowing herself to be put through that again. I suppose she wouldn't be the first though.

I'm so engrossed in my newspaper it takes me a few seconds to realise that everyone is staring at me. I clear my throat and feel my cheeks turning pink. A couple of the girls in front of me snigger, but I do my best to ignore them, closing the pages and placing the newspaper on the floor by my bag. I mutter an apology to my lecturer and pick up my pen, waiting for him to begin talking again. Once he is firmly back into his flow, I begin doodling on the paper. I figure I've missed so much already there isn't a lot of point trying to catch up now. I can see the back of Matthews head several rows in front of me and my mind starts to wander off in a different direction.

Last time we went out he was pretty mean to me, but I can't help but go running every time he calls. Matthew DeBoucier. His dad is the CEO of some huge IT company, I forget which one, and they've got a ton of money. He took me to one of their corporate events last year and our picture ended up in the society pages of *Hello!* Magazine. I framed the picture and sent a copy to my mum. She loved it. That's where I'm going to be every week pretty soon. Don't get me wrong, I don't fancy being hounded by the press constantly, like Diana is, but a little snap here and there would be nice. Mum was really pleased when I got a place at uni, told me it would be a good place to find the right sort of husband. It wasn't the reason I'd applied but she did have a good point. It's definitely the place to meet the right sort of man. She also told me to stay away from all that tree hugging and feminism nonsense. I'd laughed at the time, but you'd be surprised how much of it there is about. Especially feminism. My course is full of girls keen to argue the feminist point. Although I suppose that's pretty standard on most English courses. One of my lecturers is a bit of a hippy as well, crystals hanging around her neck and a tie dyed skirt. She'd looked absolutely horrified when I turned up to my lecture a few weeks ago in a twin set and pearls. I thought it looked elegant, she told me I was letting the side down and had I really considered the message I was sending out to men. I'd thought about asking her exactly the same question, but decided it wasn't worth the bother. Thankfully, no one else had been around to hear her little rant, how embarrassing would that have been? I like to dress conservatively. Elegant. Not like some girls you see with absolutely everything on display. And you'd never catch me in a dungarees and boots look that seems to be so in at the moment. Matthew turns around and catches my eye, giving me a wicked smile which sends the heat rushing back up to my cheeks again. Desperate to hide my face, I reach down and pick up my newspaper again, spreading it on my lap and pretending to be engrossed. Diana's face fills almost every page, the journalists analysing everything from her outfit to the choice of words used in the statement and trying to speculate over the millions of questions left unanswered.

I still can't believe she's pregnant. I wonder what that will make the baby. Obviously he or she will be half brother or sister to the heirs to the throne, is there a special name for that? If the baby is Muslim how will the

Royal Family feel about that? Maybe they'll welcome it, a sign that the country is moving with the times and open to embracing new cultures? Somehow I can't see that happening. Can you imagine the Queen exposing her family in that way? Obviously what Diana does with her life is up to her, officially, but people still see her as royalty. People still look up to her, follow her lead. I wonder if Diana is seriously considering converting. It must be hard not to get involved in something that is such a big part of your partners life, or at least show an interest. Don't Muslims not eat certain types of food? That could make meal times pretty difficult, although I suppose with the sort of money the pair of them have, eating out every night is hardly likely to be a problem. I suppose they both probably have chefs as well, people who would have to prepare two different meals if they were asked, because it's their job. That's what money can do for you.

Not everyone will happy about the baby though. Diana's mother doesn't speak to her because she started seeing that other Muslim bloke, the surgeon. I bet she's even happier now Diana is engaged to one and expecting his baby. Still, at least Dodi's father is pleased. A couple of the papers have implied that he's only so happy about the union because it will make it easier for him to get a British passport. That's so cynical. All a father wants is to see his children happy, at least that's what my dad says to me, and Dodi is clearly on top of the world. Beautiful woman by his side, expecting his baby, what's not to be happy about? I know Mohammad Al Fayed has been refused a British passport several times, and how it might seem that by his son marrying such a well loved icon could seem to be his ticket in, but I really can't believe that's how it is. Who wouldn't be thrilled that their son was marrying Diana? She's practically the perfect woman, everything most women aim to be. Everything most men want to be with.

As the lecture winds down, people begin packing books away into bags and getting to their feet. I close the paper and slide it into my bag, along with the pad of paper containing nothing except some bad doodles and my name written over and over. There are some good photos and a copy of the statement about the baby that can go in my scrap book when I get in. I'm sure I'll be able to copy notes from someone else later on. Maybe Matthew, if he wants to play nice. If he wants to take me somewhere nice. I catch his eye and smile coyly at him as I pass on my way out.

CHAPTER TWELVE

Diana covers her hair with a light blue scarf and steps gracefully down from the four by four. She looks both ways, up and down the quiet road, before donning the large dark sunglasses and making her way towards the opulent building in front of her. Diana stops, raising her gaze to take in the large bronze dome at the top of the building. Pulling her coat tightly around her against the chill in the winter wind, she tucks her gloveless hands underneath each armpit and once again makes her way towards the building in front of her. At the door, Diana stops as if afraid to continue. She looks over her shoulder at the car still purring at the curb, almost as if she is weighing up her options. Taking a deep breath, she returns her gaze to the door in front of her and with new resolve pushes open the door and steps into the mosque.

Diana stops at the threshold of the next room and bends gracefully to remove her shoes, leaving them lined up neatly behind several other pairs. She flinches slightly as she puts her feet on the cold tiled floor, protected only by a thin pair of tights. Straightening, Diana finds herself looking into a pair of deep brown eyes set into a dark and weathered face. Smiling politely, Diana extends her hand to the man, who grasps it firmly between both of his.

"Welcome, Lady, it is an honour to meet you. Please, follow me."

He drops her hand and turns around, stepping up a small step and walking through an archway. Diana follows, looking to her right as he points out the large prayer hall. Currently empty, Diana stops for a moment and takes in the plain room, her eyes wandering to the dome in the ceiling and the stack of prayer mats located all around. Smiling, her guide waits patiently for her to take it all in before motioning her to continue onward. Diana does not smile, but follows, her eyes still darting all around her. Several men who are milling around the prayer hall stop and openly stare at her, pausing in what they are doing in order to do so. Diana pulls her scarf further over her hair and checks that her sunglasses are still in place, before looking away and hurrying onwards. She is led to a plain wooden door and motioned to knock. Her hand shaking slightly, Diana raps smartly on the door and breathes deeply as she waits for a response.

"Enter."

Smiling widely at Diana, the man who escorted her grasps the brass knob of the door and pushes it inwards. He moves to the side, extending his arm to hold the door open and allow her to pass. Diana smiles weakly in response before stepping through the door, which is promptly closed behind her. Seated at a small round table, three aged men smile encouragingly at Diana, motioning at the single empty chair in encouragement. She seems momentarily rooted to the spot, staring fixatedly at the three men. Seeming to snap out of her reverie suddenly, Diana moves towards the empty chair and sits down gracefully. She smiles at the three men, a smile that doesn't quite reach to her eyes, and thanks them for taking the time to see her.

When Diana finally emerges from within the room, her smile has warmed up considerably and she is chatting amiably with the three elders as they move to escort her from the building. As they walk through the mosque once more, Diana's eyes take in the increased level of activity taking place around the building.

"It is almost time for prayer."

The elder who had done most of the talking within the room answers Diana's unspoken question.

"Islam is a community, not just a religion. We each help the other in order for things to run smoothly, we each offer the others our love and support, advice and guidance."

He looks briefly to Diana's stomach before his gaze returns to her face and he continues.

"If we can offer any further guidance to you please do not hesitate to return so we can speak further."

Having reached the outer doors once more, two of the men hold out their arms to steady Diana as she places her shoes back on her feet. Straightening herself, she clasps each of their hands in turn before addressing them all.

"Thank you for taking the time to see me, it has been truly enlightening. I think, if it is not too much trouble, that I would like to come back and meet with you further in the very near future."

The men beam at Diana and nod several times, clearly pleased that she will be returning. Smiling back, Diana makes her way to the main doors, before pausing and turning once more to thank her hosts. The three men stand in a line, smiling widely until Diana steps through the door and closes it behind her. They receive several intrigued looks from the people milling about in the mosque, but return to the privacy of their room without stopping to talk to anyone.

Outside the front of the mosque Diana tightens her headscarf against the rain that has started drizzling down from the low grey clouds. She scurries forward to the black four by four that is still waiting at the curb, despite the no parking sign displayed several hundred yards further up the road. Although the driver begins to make his way out of his seat, Diana does not wait for him to open the door for her, instead flinging it open and scrambling into the back of the car. She is smiling widely and after securing her seatbelt firmly begins to unwind her now damp scarf from around her head. Catching it several times on the arms of her large sunglasses, Diana removes them and discards both the glasses and the headscarf on the seat next to her. Smiling at the driver looking back at her in the mirror, Diana requests

"Home, please."

When Dodi arrives at Diana's home he finds her more cheerful and positive than he has seen her in many months. Dressed to impress, Diana compliments Dodi on his classic black tuxedo. The pair are due to attend a charity event for the hospital Diana visited after the engagement was announced, but Diana is not yet dressed, nor making any attempt to be. She motions Dodi to sit next to her on the bed, where she waits cross legged like an eager child. Dodi, a puzzled look on his face, makes his way to the bed, where he perches on the edge, careful not to crease his suit. Diana reaches out and takes his hand

"I went to visit a mosque today."

Dodi looks puzzled and waits for Diana to continue.

"Not officially, privately. I went to talk with the elders there."

Diana takes a deep breath before continuing on to explain herself.

"I wanted to get some perspective on our situation. I know you've tried to explain it to me, and so has your father, but I wanted clarification. Plus I know that if we were seen to be doing something wrong that you would try to keep it from me, to protect me."

Diana smiles with genuine affection at her fiancé, before continuing.

"I called and spoke to the Imam at the mosque; did you know there was one in Kensington? Anyway, he agreed to meet me for a chat and so I went there this morning. We talked for almost an hour, him and two others, and they showed me around. We didn't really go into any details about anything, but they were very welcoming and said I could come back any time I liked to talk more."

The words rush out of her mouth in almost one long stream before coming to an abrupt halt, Diana beams at Dodi, who is still sitting on the edge of the bed looking slightly bemused.

"Darling, that's wonderful, but do you think we could possibly discuss it a little later on, seeing as we're due to arrive at this fundraiser in less than an hour?"

Diana's face falls, her excited eyes sink to the floor, subdued like a child after a telling off.

"I only wanted to show you I was taking an interest."

Her voice has a definite pout in it and Dodi's smile widens as he takes her hand.

"And I'm thrilled darling, really I am, but I know how much this charity means to you and how much you would hate to be late. Maybe we could sit down later and you could tell me all about it?"

Diana's smile returns to her face as she leans forward and kisses Dodi on the cheek. Hopping nimbly off of the bed she makes her way to the bathroom, stopping and smiling at him affectionately over her shoulder before closing the door behind her.

Diana takes Dodi's outstretched arm and makes her way out of the limousine. She smiles warmly at the photographers and poses patiently with Dodi's hand on her stomach whilst they snap away. It is a cold night and Diana shivers slightly at the chill in the air and pulls her warm wrap tighter around her. Her face is flushed and her eyes look bright and excited for the first time in weeks. Dodi slips and arm around her and pulls her close, whispering in her ear

"I think we've given them enough for now."

Diana smiles her agreement, before turning and waving goodbye to the photographers as the pair begin to make their way into the building.

The event stretches late into the night and eventually Diana and Dodi excuse themselves, citing tiredness on Diana's part. The pair have been showered with compliments and best wishes all evening and both of them are still wearing beaming smiles. Making their way out to the car waiting, Dodi stops Diana, circling both his arms around her waist

"You looked radiant tonight. I heard several people comment on how well you looked. Pregnancy suits you."

Diana smiles coyly and reaches up to kiss Dodi softly on the lips. The chill of the night breaks their embrace as Diana shudders softly at the wind, and the pair continue on the way to the car. They nod to the driver, who is waiting with the door, and both of them slide effortlessly into the soft leather seats. Diana laughs to herself.

"I suppose that will start getting difficult pretty soon."

Dodi leans over and kisses her softly again as the driver begins to pull out into the traffic. Breaking the embrace, Diana reaches round and fastens her seatbelt tightly, before reaching out and taking Dodi's hand. Once he is firmly strapped in she leans over and rests her head on his shoulders, smiling as she closes her eyes.

The ringing of the phone wakes her and for a moment she looks around, as if unsure of where she is. Her dress is hanging neatly on the back of the door and her shoes and bag are on the floor beneath it. Diana smiles as she hears the sound of the shower running and reaches out to pick up the persistent phone.

"His Royal Highness, Prince Charles, would like to speak with you."

The voice at the end of the line is clipped, its tone almost rude. Diana responds in kind.

"Put him on."

"He requests a meeting. Three o'clock this afternoon. A car will pick you up."

Before Diana can respond there is a click and the line goes dead. She is still holding the receiver when Dodi emerges from the shower and looks at her questioningly. She hangs up before she responds

"Charles would like to speak to me, apparently. He's sending a car this afternoon."

"Do you know why?"

Dodi moves around the room slowly, continuing with getting dressed as he speaks

"I haven't got a clue. The baby maybe? Or our engagement? Or both."

"It's none of his business."

Dodi's tone turns colder as he looks at Diana

"Don't be like that. I know it's none of his business, but it's not like we weren't expecting that he would have something to say on the matter."

"Do you want me there?"

Dodi resumes getting dressed as he speaks

"No, it's ok. Nothing I can't handle. Can't imagine it will take too long anyway."

Dodi walks up to the bed, takes Diana's hand and kisses her gently

"I have to go to work, but I'll be at the end of the phone if you need me."

Diana smiles in response and holds on to Dodi's hand as he begins to leave the room, dropping it as their arms stretch out.

"Love you."

"Love you too."

Still smiling, Diana dresses and makes her way down to breakfast. She helps herself to coffee and toast laid out on the table and declines when one of her staff asks if she requires anything preparing for her. Diana sips on her coffee and unfolds the newspaper that has been laid out next to her coffee cup. She smiles at the photograph of her and Dodi that graces the front page, before taking in the headline.

"Princess Diana Converting to Islam?"

Her eyes widen in panic, and flick to the tiny column of writing at the bottom left hand corner of the page. In bold letters at the bottom she is advised "For full story turn to pages four and five." Diana hurriedly leafs through the paper before stopping suddenly. Splashed across pages four and five are photographs of Diana leaving the mosque, heavily disguised. In the centre of page five, a candid snap of Diana in the car catches her removing her scarf and dark glasses, smiling broadly. Diana groans quietly to herself, lowering her head until it touches the table and mutters to herself

"No wonder Charles wants to talk to me."

CHAPTER THIRTEEN

When the car pulls up outside the door at exactly three o'clock, Diana is already waiting. Dressed in head to toe black, she eschews her usual facial cover-ups and steps outside to meet her ex husband. Charles does not get out from the car, instead the door is held open for Diana by the driver, who does not make eye contact with her. Closing the door behind her, the driver hurries back to the front of the car and starts the engine. When Charles speaks, it is firstly to the driver.

"Just drive please Malcolm, somewhere quiet."

Diana has settled into the seat opposite Charles in the large car and fastens her seatbelt tightly. She clears her throat, showing her annoyance at being ignored.

"Diana, you're looking well."

Diana smiles a limp smile in response

"Can we just say what needs to be said? We've both got very busy schedules."

Charles tucks his hands into his lap, his face calm and placid. His tone is carefully polite and he speaks slowly as if every word is well chosen.

"There is no need for us to forget the pleasantries. Still, we do have rather a lot to talk about."

Diana looks directly at Charles, who avoids her gaze, and waits for him to continue.

"Your relationship with Dodi Al Fayed...."

"Is none of your business."

Diana voice is measured and even, her eyes still boring into Charles. He raises his head and meets her gaze, waiting for a few moments before responding in a low voice.

"Not on a personal level, no. But as my former wife and mother to the heirs to the throne you are still seen by many people as part of the Royal Family. I would expect you to understand this and conduct yourself as such."

Charles voice has taken on a condescending, cutting tone. He and Diana stare at each other for several minutes as his words sink in, with Diana taking several deep breaths before responding

"And exactly which part of the relationship is it that you disprove of?"

Her voice shakes with repressed anger and furious tears pool in her eyes. Charles stares back at her, his face matching his condescending tone and reaches down to offer her a tissue from the drinks cabinet concealed in the car. Diana ignores the offer, instead reaching into her handbag and producing a tissue of her own. She dabs at her eyes, refusing to let the moisture escape, as Charles continues.

"Of course, no one would presume to tell you how to live your life...."

A small laugh escapes from Diana's lips and Charles stares at her coldly for a moment before continuing

"As I was saying, I do not presume to tell you how to conduct your life, only to remember that you are still part of the royal image and as such you still represent the Royal Family."

His voice is cold and once again Charles avoids Diana's gaze. Her eyes now dry, Diana presses him to continue.
"Go on."

There is a sharp edge to her tone and a wary looks flashes momentarily across Charles face, erasing itself almost instantly as he continues
"The sudden engagement after the accident was a bit of a shock, but we offered our congratulations and wished you all the best. A few eyebrows were raised about the out of wedlock pregnancy, rumours' flying about that the baby was the reason for the shock engagement, and yet we kept a dignified silence. Then in the newspaper this morning the entire country reads that you're converting to Islam. Do I need to remind you that the Queen, your ex mother in law and your sons grandmother, is Head of the Church of England? How do you think it will look if a member of her, albeit extended, family, turns her back on that religion? Begins looking elsewhere for spiritual satisfaction? Now, I have no idea if this is one of your whims or if your fiancé..."

Charles all but spits out the word
"...has put you up to this, but I'm telling you now that it has to stop. You will speak to the press immediately and deny all accusations that you are turning away from the Church of England. Give them some other reason for your being at a mosque, make it up if you have to."

Diana stares at Charles for a moment, her pink lips parted slightly and a crimson flush building on her cheeks
"I'll do nothing of the sort."

The volume and venom of her voice seems to shock even Diana as the words spill from her mouth. Charles flinches before looking to the driver as if concerned about what he should overhear. Before he can respond Diana starts again
"When we got divorced you gave up any right to dictate to me what I may and may not do. You, and the rest of your family. Yes, I am still the mother to two very important children, but as long as they are well cared for and well brought up I do not see how any decisions I make in my private life have any reflection on them, or you for that matter."

Diana's hands are curled into fists in her lap and she is physically shaking.
"How dare you summon me from my home in an attempt to illustrate to me the *proper* way for me to live my life? How dare you presume to think that you can just snap your fingers and command that I stop behaving in a way that you disapprove of, because of some imagined negative reflection on you?"

Diana shifts in her seat, turning her back on Charles, and addresses the driver
"Take me home Malcolm, please."

The driver looks in his rear view mirror for confirmation from Charles, who ignores him and addresses Diana once more.

"I knew that you were going to be difficult about this. If nothing else, think of William and Harry and what your behaviour is doing to them."

Diana's eyes flash in temper and she practically screams in response
"My boys are pleased to finally see me happy."

Her emphasis on the word finally causes Charles to flinch and he sinks back in his seat, signalling to his driver with a lazy flick of his fingers. They spend the journey back to Diana's home in silence, Diana staring resolutely out of the window while Charles makes notes in a battered black diary that he retrieves from the inner pocket of his suit jacket. When the car finally pulls up outside Diana's house, she undoes her seatbelt and lets it recoil noisily back into place before beginning to move towards the door. She does not wait for the driver, instead attempting to open the door herself. Charles grabs her gently by the wrist and she turns and meets his gaze, before looking pointedly down at her arm. Charles lets go swiftly, but implores her
"Please think about what I've said."

Diana keeps her eyes locked with her former husband for several seconds before turning and exiting the car without responding. She does not look back as she walks towards her front door, but her shoulders relax from their tensed position as soon as she hears the car begin to pull away.
    Inside the house Diana makes her way to the kitchen and pours herself a cup of coffee. Shooing away any offers of help, she rummages in the fridge and in the

cupboards before wandering off with a pile of biscuits and chocolate tucked under her arms and settles into the living room. The staff all exchange concerned looks, but begin to go about their normal tasks in an effort to leave Diana undisturbed. Kicking off her shoes, Diana settles on the sofa with her armful of goodies and tucks her feet beneath her. She takes a long drink from her coffee and leans back with her eyes closed, one hand rubbing at her temple. Several minutes pass like this before the ringing of the phone interrupts her reverie. Moments after it stops Diana is disturbed once again, this time by a timid knock on the door. Her mouth crammed full of biscuit, Diana takes more coffee in an attempt to wash it down, before managing to call out in a muffled tone

"Come in."

The door opens slowly and one of the housekeepers enters, her feet shuffling and her eyes glued to a spot several feet in front of Diana. Diana clears her throat in an effort to prompt the girl to speak

"Mr Al Fayed is on the phone for you Ma'am."

The girls voice is barely audible and she fiddles with her hands, clearly nervous about disturbing her employer.

Diana mumbles a thank you in response and the girl scurries from the room, evidently glad to be leaving. Breaking several pieces of chocolate from a bar, Diana moves slowly towards the telephone in the room, settling herself down on the chair closest to it and placing a chunk of chocolate in her mouth before picking up the handset.

"Hello?"

The words are slurred, the melting chocolate slowing their release from Diana's mouth.

"Diana?"

Diana swallows her mouthful and washes it down with a mouthful of lukewarm coffee before replying

"Yes, Dodi, who did you think it was?"

There is a hint of impatience in her voice which Dodi picks up on.

"I'm sorry, am I interrupting?"

Diana breathes in and out several times before she speaks

"No, no, sorry. I was just having five minutes to myself."

"Was it that bad?"

Diana stuffs another piece of chocolate into her mouth and answers Dodi's question with a question of her own

"Have you seen the paper?"

"I have. I tried to call as soon as I saw it but I've been waylaid with meetings all day. I presume that was what Charles wanted to talk about?"

"Of course it was. Apparently he can only ignore so much of my *behaviour* before he feels the need to intervene and set my life back on the appropriate course."

"My god, that man has a bloody cheek. Did you tell him it was none of his business how you decide to live your life?"

Dodi does not raise his voice, but anger resonates from the receiver regardless. Diana attempts to pacify him

"You have to see it from his point of view. I am the mother to the heirs of the throne; it is all about public appearances. But yes, I did tell him it was none of his business."

"And so there would be something wrong with you converting to Islam?"

Diana has done nothing to pacify Dodi, if anything he seems angrier

"Well, it would probably cause quite a scandal."

Her tone is soothing, but Dodi seems to be getting more worked up with every word

"So they still feel they can tell you what to do, dictate to you how you live your life. Are you going to allow them to keep you from the path of enlightenment?"

"Hold on Dodi, I haven't made any decisions either way yet. I went to the mosque to learn, only the newspapers are saying that I'm going to convert. Both you and Charles should know better than to believe what you read in the papers."

Dodi begins to speak but Diana cuts him off

"And believe me when I say that any decisions I make in my life, any at all, will be completely my own. I won't allow Charles or any other member of that family to pressure me into anything."

Dodi breathes a sigh of relief

"That makes me feel much better."

"Any decision I make will be because it is what is best for me, because it is what makes me happy. Don't think

I'll be letting you influence or pressure me in any way either."

Dodi tries to respond, but Diana hangs up the phone, settles back in her chair closes her eyes and places another piece of chocolate in her mouth. When the phone rings again, Diana picks up the handset and places it on the table without speaking, before leaning back in her chair and closing her eyes.

CHAPTER FOURTEEN

So I got talking to this Muslim girl at school, Jameela. She's in a couple of my lectures, doesn't really talk to anyone and always makes loads of notes. I caught up with her after class the other day and asked if I could borrow what she'd written as I'd missed some stuff. She'd looked pretty sceptical but handed them over once I'd offered to buy her a cup of coffee in return. When I'd got them home her notes were extensive, it looked like she'd practically copied down every word the lecturer said. I started to read through them but it was taking forever, so I nipped down to the library and photocopied them. Anyway, when I met her the next day to give them back, I took her for a cup of coffee as promised and after we'd been talking about school for a bit I gently broached the subject of religion. It was pretty easy to bring up actually, with all the stuff about Diana around. I guess Jameela isn't used to being able to talk about it much because she went on for ages and into loads of detail. She seemed pretty excited I was showing an interest actually, she went from being sceptical about having coffee with me to practically my best friend in about ten seconds flat. I was worried at first about asking something that would offend her, or having her think I was only taking an interest because it was 'trendy', but she was totally cool about it. She said her Imam, I think that's the word she used, had given a talk on how people might show a new level of interest in Islam and how they should all do their best to educate people. Jameela said that she hadn't paid much attention, didn't really believe it, but that she was really excited to be able to go back and tell him that he was right. She went on a bit though, about all the do's and don'ts. I tried complimenting her outfit once, just for a bit of change of pace in the conversation, but that just came back to religion and how it is right for a woman to remain as covered as possible. Still, at least she was wearing a beautiful, fashionable cover up. Anyway, she invited me to the mosque with her today, so I can meet this man who is so interested in bringing Islam to the western world. Apparently he can answer any of my questions much better than she can, so I agreed to go. I guess that's probably what Diana did really, show an interest for Dodi and make the effort to find out about his religion. I've tried to emulate her outfit, because I was really struggling to work out what I'm supposed to wear. I know I've got to be covered up as much as possible, which isn't too hard because it's freezing outside, so I've put on a nice pair of trousers and a plain, long sleeved jumper with a shirt underneath. Kept the jewellery and make up to a minimum too, you know, I'm not there to impress anyone. It's purely about finding out about a different type of spiritual path. Although if there are any wealthy, good looking young men there it wouldn't be the worst thing in the world.

I had arranged to meet Jameela outside the mosque at 11am, but after missing the bus I was running about fifteen minutes late. She looked pretty cold and pissed off, but she didn't say anything, just took me inside and told me where I could hang my coat up. I watched as she took her shoes off and left them in a pile with many others, before following suit, glad I'd put tights on underneath my trousers as the floor was freezing. I followed Jameela through an archway and we stepped through into a large, almost bare hall. She pointed out the large dome in the ceiling and told me it used to be used to help magnify the speakers words, but that now they used microphones so it was mostly decorative. Mats were laid out on the floor, each one different but all pointing in the same direction. Jameela explained that they were prayer mats and were pointed in the direction of Mecca, the holy city. The whole time she was speaking it was in hushed tones, and although people milled about here and there, the whole place was practically silent, like a church really. It had the same holy feel about it, like your every word, even your every thought, had best be good because God was watching. Or Allah, should I say. We talked a bit about the towers in the mosque as well. Minarets, I think she called them, and how they were used for calling people to prayer. It's such a dedicated religion, with a certain time for everything. Not like Christianity which, apart from Sundays, has a general do as much as you like whenever you like kind of feel to it. Although maybe that's just my impression of it. Mum had a little phase where she took me to Sunday school for about six months, but she stopped after I made enough of a fuss. It wasn't even that I didn't enjoy it when I was there, just felt like the sort of thing I should make a fuss about doing. You don't seem to get that here. Jameela talks about her religion like it's something she should be proud of, without coming across as preachy. She acts like she's so grateful to be allowed to be part of it, rather than trying to explain to me why I'm missing out because I'm not. I got a couple of funny stares from some of the people about in the mosque, though I can understand that. I suppose it's not often they get white people in here, let alone a young white girl. A couple of people smiled though, which I thought was nice. Jameela took me and introduced me to some of the elders at the mosque, which threw me a little bit. I'd thought she was just going to show me around the place and tell me what I needed to know, maybe smile and nod to the important people. She explained to them that I'd shown an interest and she'd thought of the talk given the other day and invited me along to have a look around. There were three of them, all sat round this little wooden table, deep in discussion. Jameela had dragged me to stand by the table and patiently waited for them to finish talking before introducing me. They were all pretty old, wearing those long tunic things that look like dresses, two in black and one in white. I'd smiled and shaken each of their hands and opened my mouth to decline when they asked me to sit down but Jameela practically shoved me into the seat before plonking herself next to me. Two of the men, the one in white and one of the ones in black, asked lots of questions about me. Where I came from, what I was studying, how I'd been brought up. The other one in black just sat there scowling, occasionally sniffing at something I'd said. I got the impression that he didn't want me there, that I wasn't welcome. If it hadn't been for the other two I'd have been totally intimidated by his attitude, but they put me at ease. After about twenty minutes of talking they sent the miserable one to go and make tea, something he didn't look to happy about but they must have outranked him or something because he did it without saying anything.

When Jameela and I left the mosque she was practically walking on air. Turns out even getting a smile from the three elders was difficult at times, without getting to sit and talk and have tea with them. I was feeling a bit nonplussed by the whole thing if I'm honest, I mean it wasn't a bad way to spend a few hours and I certainly learnt a lot, but I'm not sure I could do it every week. And I'm not sure I could display the level of enthusiasm Jameela seems to be displaying. It was nice to feel like I was part of something important for a few hours, but at the same time I was pretty conscious of the fact that I stuck out like a sore thumb, and of the fact that not everyone wanted me there. I'm not sure if that's something that would get better over time though, or if it would always be there. Everyone drummed into me today how Islam is a community, a family. It would be horrible to never feel like I was properly part of it, to always be the black sheep. Before we left the elder in white gave me a copy of the Qur'an to look at and told me I was always welcome. The book is sitting on my desk now, I've had a bit of a look through it but I think I'd need help understanding it properly. Muslim kids have lessons on it from a really young age apparently, can you imagine if I had to go and sit with a class of school kids once a week for lessons? How embarrassing would that be? Jameela offered to help me with it when we were walking back, I'd said I'd talk to her about it in our next class together. It's a lot to take on board and not the sort of decision you can make lightly. What if I convert and then realise that it's not for me? Can you just say 'whoops I made a mistake' and not go anymore? Somehow it doesn't really strike me as working that way. And what about Christianity? I know I'm not exactly a model Christian, but can I just say 'sorry God, it's you and Jesus I want to worship really.' And be a Christian again?

I'm going out with Matthew tonight. I don't think I'll be telling him about my little trip to the mosque, I don't think he'd understand. He's the sort of bloke who thinks something is wrong just because it's different or he doesn't understand it. I don't know what converting would mean for our relationship either, what little relationship we have. I guess inter religion relationships must be ok for Diana and Dodi to have one, but then maybe not seeing as she's converting. I know the papers are just saying that she might at the moment, but I think she will. I think Dodi would want a proper Muslim family and I think Diana wants to give it to him. The subject came up briefly at the mosque today actually, something was said about how the baby would have to be a Muslim. I can't imagine Diana being happy with her baby having a different religion to her although if she cconverts I can't see William and Harry suddenly turning Muslim too. Can you just picture their conversation with Charles and the Queen? I bet neither of them are happy about Diana's planned conversion, so I'd imagine they'd take it even worse if the boys wanted to follow in her footsteps. Still, everyone should have the right to make their own decisions, that's what I think. Not that I have a clue what I'm going to do. Except go back to the mosque next week. Because I promised Jameela that I would.

CHAPTER FIFTEEN

Diana stands on the platform and braces herself against the chill wind. Wrapped up in a warm, faux fur coat, and hat and gloves firmly in place, she smiles and waves at the crowd assembled. Dodi wraps his arm snug around her waist and motions for her to follow him as he makes his way towards the boat gently bobbing on the murky water of the river Thames. The pair move forward slowly, stopping to make small talk and smile for the people who have turned up to see them. Diana's small clutch bag slips suddenly from beneath her arm and she untangles herself from Dodi's embrace to retrieve it. As she bends low, a bullet whistles through the gap between the two, passing right through where Diana would have been standing before embedding itself into the hull of the boat behind them. There is absolute silence for a moment, Diana seems frozen in position half way towards picking her bag up. Someone in the crowd screams and the rest of the people gathered seem to break out of their reverie. Several more screams pierce through the air and send the security gathered bursting into action. Most of Diana and Dodi's private teams, plus the security stationed at the event all begin to dash towards the general area the shot seems to have been fired from, whilst the rest of the team with Diana begin to attempt to bundle her back into the car she arrived in. Still seemingly frozen in place, Dodi practically scoops

Diana up, declining any help from the remaining bodyguards gathered around them. She lays in his arms like a child until they reach the door of the car, upon sight of which Diana begins to violently thrash and scream. Dodi mutters to her softly, holding her close to him and kissing the top of her head as he continues to try and place her in the car. Her tantrum refusing to abate, Dodi finally motions to two of the men surrounding them to help him into the car. Reaching for Diana's legs, the taller of the suited men is dealt a swift kick to the jaw which sends him momentarily reeling. Taking note, the other man wraps his strong arms around Diana's legs and motions for Dodi to continue trying to get into the car. Finally through the doors, Dodi straps the seatbelt around the pair of them and positions Diana's head in his lap. Although her thrashing has subsided, she is still whimpering and her face has taken on the ashy pallor that has become all too familiar recently. Slamming the door behind them, the security team bang on the roof to signal the driver to start moving, before returning to their own vehicle to follow closely behind. Steering the car easily into the traffic, the driver looks into the rear view mirror and asks in a timid voice

Where to, Sir?"

Dodi seems shocked to be spoken to, almost as if he has forgotten where he is or that input is expected from him. Shaking his head softly and looking down at Diana he replies

"The hospital, I suppose."

Dodi paces anxiously outside of the room while the doctors look over Diana. He checks his watch again and again, his face showing more concern as time passes. At the end of the corridor the lift doors open with a ping and four men in dark suits make their way out. Dodi turns to greet his security team, keen to know the latest news.

"Mr Al Fayed, I'm sorry to tell you that we were unable to locate the shooter."

Dodi's face drops as he hears the report and he looks again to the room where Diana is being examined.

"Did you find anything? Was anyone else hurt?"

"There have been no other reported injuries and no reports of any other shots being fired. It appears that either you or Lady Diana were the intended target. If she had not moved when she did the bullet would have hit her right between the eyes. She's a very lucky lady."

Dodi grimaces as he replies

"That remains to be seen. What now?"

The man speaking shifts uncomfortably

"The police have been to the scene, but have been unable to locate any evidence. They are waiting to see if any terrorist groups step forward to take responsibility for the attack. Until then I suggest we increase the security around both of you and keep public appearances to a minimum until an arrest has been made."

Dodi nods morosely and turns his back on the team, who begin to move themselves into various positions along the corridor. The sound of the door to Diana's room opening causes Dodi's head to snap up and he looks immediately to the doctor leaving the room. He answers Dodi's unspoken question

"She's physically fine, as is the baby. However she is in quite a deep state of shock. We have given her a mild sedative, just to calm her down and she's sleeping at the moment. When she wakes up it will be fine for you to take her home, as long as she has round the clock care for a few days. Obviously we'd recommend as much rest as possible and to try and keep her away from stressful situations."

The doctor tucks his clipboard under his arm and is on his way up the corridor before Dodi can say anything. Peeking his head into the door, he stares at Diana's ashen pallor. Dark circles have formed underneath her eyes and with the bed sheet pulled up to her chin she could easily be mistaken for a body on the way to the morgue. Only the faint rise and fall of her chest illustrates the fact that she is still alive. Dodi stares at her for a few more moments before turning round and motioning to the closest member of the security team.

"I want you in there with her. No one goes in except for me or a doctor. You will not leave, not even to go to the bathroom. Do you understand?"

The man nods once and moves into position, standing at the end of Diana's bed. Dodi closes the door on them, a tear falling down his cheek as he turns away.

It is dark when Diana wakes and for a moment she looks around the room as if confused about where she is. Dodi is slumped in the chair next to the bed, dozing, and a member of the security team waits alert at the end of the bed. As she struggles into a sitting position, Dodi rouses and takes her hand

"Diana, are you ok? Do you feel all right? Can I get you anything?"

She shakes her head slowly as if trying to clear it, before responding with a question of her own
"How long have I been here?"

Dodi checks his watch, squinting in the dark
"About twelve hours. They gave you a sedative to calm you down. We thought you'd be awake sooner than this. You can go home in the morning."

She slumps forwards, resting her head in her hands and breaths deeply for a few moments
"Someone shot at us."

She sounds unsure, as if she cannot trust her own memory of what happened. Dodi hesitates before responding.
"At the boat launch. Yes."
"Did they catch them?"

Diana stares at Dodi hopefully, her face falling when she sees his expression
"Several terrorist organisations have claimed responsibility, but the police are reluctant to believe any of them."

She looks at him suspiciously and waits for him to continue
"Most of them are extremist Islamic groups, unhappy about our relationship, the fact that we're having a baby or the fact that the papers are convinced that you're converting to Islam."

"Or all three."

Diana has a bitter tone in her voice. She looks to Dodi, who avoids her gaze and stares at the floor.
"What happened to me?"

Dodi responds without looking up
"The doctors said you went into shock. You were very lucky to have moved when you did. They sedated you and wanted to observe you for a while. The baby is fine."

Diana places her hand over her stomach and looks down at it. The pair sit in silence for a moment, before Diana speaks again
"What have the police said?"

Dodi sighs and stands up, pacing around the room. The bodyguard in the room is careful to avoid his gaze and does his best to appear like a statue as the couple talk.
"The police don't know what to think, who to believe. There was no evidence at the scene and the shooter was long gone by the time anyone got there..."

Dodi aims a sneer in the direction of the bodyguard, who does his best to ignore it
"For the time being we are both to have maximum security at all times and to refrain from making any unnecessary public appearances. And the doctor said that you had to get as much rest as possible."

Diana begins to pull the sheets off of her legs, struggling as she hurries. Dodi stares at her for a moment before asking

"Where are you going?"

Diana stops in her tracks, staring at Dodi in incredulity

"I'm going home. I'm not going to sit here and wait around for something to happen. I'd rather be in my own home. I'd feel safer at home."

"Diana, it's the middle of the night. Couldn't you at least wait until morning?"

Diana swings both of her legs off of the bed and places her feet on the floor. She takes several deep breaths before attempting to stand, clutching on to Dodi's arm as she wobbles slightly.

"No. I want to go home now. I want to sleep in my bed and in the morning I want to speak to my boys."

She begins to gather up her things from around the room, before throwing her coat on over the hospital gown and making for the door. Dodi remains rooted to the spot as she flings open the door and marches out into the hallway. The bodyguard wavers for a moment, before following her, leaving Dodi alone in the room. He breathes deeply twice before following after them, running slightly to avoid missing the lift that they had piled into along with the rest of the security team. No one speaks as the lift descends slowly to the ground floor. When the doors ping open the security team burst into action, checking the area is clear. Dodi and Diana wait in front of the now closed doors for the sweep to be complete, before walking towards the exit. Neither of them speak, but Diana does not complain when Dodi wraps his arm around her against the freezing cold once they make their way through the sliding doors. Several photographers are waiting out in the cold despite the hour and hurry forward to catch a shot of Diana. Before they have a chance to snap, Dodi and the security team form a tight circle around her, protecting her from their intrusion. They move forward as a pack, bundling Diana into the car that has seemingly appeared from nowhere. The cameras begin to flash in vain, the photographers grasping at the slightest chance of a picture, before the door closes and Diana drives off into the night.

CHAPTER SIXTEEN

Diana wraps the duvet cover around herself and stares forlornly at the television. Brought into her room to offer some entertainment while she follows the doctor's orders to get some rest, the bulky appliance stands out in stark contrast to the delicate feel of the rest of the decor. Propping her body up on her elbows, Diana flicks through the channels again and again, watching her own face appearing more often than anything else. She had watched the news out of morbid curiosity first thing in the morning, and stared horrified as one of the TV crew camera captured a shot of just how close the bullet had come to hitting her. Diana had turned the TV off after that, alternating between reading and dozing to fill her time. Dodi had left strict instructions with the staff that she was to get as much rest as possible, and so all of her commitments had been cancelled and Diana had been practically ordered to bed. Disappointment clear in her face at seeing that accounts of the assassination attempt are still all over the news, Diana flicks the set off with the remote and drops back down onto her pillows. Reaching over for her book, she throws it down in frustration before moving back into a sitting position. Kicking with her legs and pulling at the covers, Diana manages to free herself from the bed and swings her legs over the edge. Feet sinking into the plush carpet, she smiles a small self satisfied smile and begins to make her way towards the bedroom door.

The corridor is empty and Diana's bare feet make no noise as she travels towards the stairs. Avoiding the main staircase that leads out into the hall, she opts instead for the lesser used back staircase that will take her practically into the kitchen. Robe wrapped around her and hair dishevelled from spending the better part of the day in bed, she appears a million miles away from her usual well groomed self. Diana catches a glimpse of herself in the mirror and seems all too aware of the fact, turning away from her reflection and grimacing. Making her way towards the swing door that leads to the kitchen, Diana waits momentarily as the sound of several voices float through to her.

"It's got to be one of those terrorist groups they keep mentioning on the telly. No one else would have it in for her except them."

The voice is female, the tone hushed and conspiratorial. An older, still female voice responds

"They don't like interlopers, do they? A bit hypocritical if you ask me. It's all right for them to come and do as they please, but heaven forbid someone would go and have a nose around at what they're doing."

"It's a bit much though, trying to kill her, don't you think? Especially with her having the baby and all. I mean, who'd try to kill an innocent baby, 'specially over something as petty as religion?"

"There have been a lot of wars over religion love, not everyone sees it as petty."

There is a heavy sigh from both voices, before the sound of a door closing signals the end of the conversation. Diana pushes her way through the swing doors, careful not to make eye contact with the woman remaining in the room. She moves towards the fridge, helping herself to an apple, before taking a glass from the cupboard and heading towards the sink. The elder of the two speakers, a large middle aged woman who has been staring at Diana with her mouth open suddenly springs into action, words gushing from her mouth like water from a tap.

"Ma'am you're supposed to be resting, here let me take that for you. I can make you something proper to eat? Or some tea, perhaps you'd like some tea?"

She takes the glass from Diana's hand and pours water from the tap into it. Her hand shakes as she passes it back, water sloshing down the sides. Diana still avoids eye contact, and taking the glass and her apple, leaves the room from the same door she came in from without uttering a word.

The apple is half gone by the time Diana is back in her room, and the water glass empty. Avoiding the bed, Diana makes her way to the velvet backed chair in front of her vanity table and stares at her dishevelled reflection. Placing the apple and the glass on the table, Diana picks up a hair brush and begins running it through her unruly hair. She applies expensive moisturiser to her face, taking time to massage it in before spending time filing her nails. The reflection in the mirror stares back at her, hair still matted and unruly, skin still sallow and pale. Diana begins to cry.

When Dodi comes into the room he finds Diana in the same position he had left her in that morning, slumped in the centre of the bed. Had it not been for the disarray around her vanity table and the discarded snack it would be easy to assume that she had stayed there all day. Dodi leans over the bed and seems surprised to find Diana's eyes open, her gaze fixed on a nondescript point on the wall in front of her.

"Diana? Are you ok?"

Diana blinks several times and stares at Dodi as if she is surprised to see him there.

"What? Oh, yes, I'm fine. Just bored. It's been a long day."

Dodi sits down next to her on the bed and places his hand affectionately on her arm

"It's understandable if you're not ok. You've been through a lot. Maybe we should arrange for you to have someone come over who you can talk to?"

"I'm not crazy."

Diana spits the words out at Dodi, rising to a sitting position as she says them

"Someone tried to kill me. Twice. And you think I need therapy? What I need is some security. Someone to take care of me. Not put me on bloody house arrest while they disappear for the day."

For a moment Dodi looks as if Diana has slapped him

"Disappear? Diana, I've been working. I can't drop everything just like that because you tell me to. I can't stay here and play nursemaid just because you're feeling sorry for yourself."

"Someone tried to kill me"

Diana shrieks the words, grabbing a pillow off of the bed and flinging it at Dodi who catches it easily. Before he can respond she starts again.

"And in case you hadn't noticed I'm *supposed* to be your fiancé. I'm carrying your baby. The least you could do is care about my safety. Care whether I live or die."

Diana struggles off of the bed and flounces to the bathroom, slamming the door hard behind her. Dodi spends a moment gathering himself, before walking to the door and knocking gently.

"Diana?"

Muffled sobs and sniffs filter through the closed door, followed by the sound of a nose being blown loudly.

"Diana, I'm sorry that you're upset. I do care about your safety. I only want the best for you and the baby. You know that."

Dodi waits for a moment, his hand leaning against the door. When she does not respond he tries again

"I'll see if I can take some time off over the next couple of days. Spend some time with you while you rest. And maybe I could come with you when you next make a trip to the mosque?"

Diana flings the door open, almost causing Dodi to lose his balance

"Are you insane? I'm not supposed to be going anywhere at all for the foreseeable future and here you are suggesting a joint trip to the mosque? It's being in a relationship with a Muslim man and being seen exploring the Muslim way of life that almost got me killed."

"So what Diana? You're not going to the mosque again? You're not even going to consider Islam, simply because you're afraid? Or is this your way of telling me that our relationships over because of one nutcase who's got it in for us?"

"I didn't...I don't...."

Diana falters, as if unsure what to say. Dodi's voice softens

"You were so excited the other day, after your trip to the mosque. I really thought that your exploration of Islam would be something we could share. And of course I was hoping that we would be teaching the baby about Islam together."

Pacified by the soothing tone of Dodi's voice, Diana's head snaps up at the last comment and her eyes flash

"We haven't decided what religion the baby will be."

Dodi looks stunned for a moment

"Of course the baby will be Muslim. Did you think I was going to let you bring it up any other way? It's up to you what you do with your life, but my child will be raised into Islam."

"Don't you dare presume to dictate to me what *our* child will or will not be. I am the child's mother and I will decide what is best for them."

There is venom in Diana's voice and she steps back from the threshold of the bathroom door and slams it, the solid wood barely missing Dodi's nose. He steps back from the door, hands resting either side of the frame and lays his head forward. Lashing out, his toe connects hard with the bottom of the door and it shakes in response. Dodi pushes against the doorframe, using the momentum to turn his back on the bathroom and Diana, before striding across the room and flinging the bedroom door open. It bounces off of the wall as he marches out into the corridor and down the main stairway.

Slumped on the floor in the bathroom, her back against the side of the bath, Diana sobs quietly. One hand positioned against her temple, the other rests against her slightly protruding belly. The sound of the front door slamming reaches all the way up the stairs and the volume of Diana's sobbing increases. She reaches for a tissue and blows her nose noisily, before discarding the tissue down the toilet and reaching for another. As her hysterics increase, Diana begins to retch, moving herself to the toilet bowl just in time for the water and apple to resurface. Tears stream down her cheeks as she vomits until there is nothing left to come, before slumping back down onto the cold floor.

It is hours later when Diana awakes and the bathroom is cold and dark. She shudders and begins to gather herself up from the floor, moving awkwardly. Without turning the light on she moves to the sink, avoiding looking in the mirror as she fills a glass up with water and washes out her mouth. Spitting the water out, Diana refills the glass and drinks deeply. The glass finished, she holds on to the edge of the sink for several minutes, breathing slowly, before standing tall and walking into the well lit bedroom. Diana's face, a carefully composed mask of indifference, falls as she scans the room and sees that it is empty. Dinner has been left for her, carefully covered to retain as much heat as possible. Diana walks over to the little table and places her hand on the metal dish cover. Finding it stone cold she abandons it and makes her way back to the bed. Reaching out to the telephone table, she picks up the receiver and holds it to her ear, listening to the dial tone. Diana reaches out to dial, her hand faltering at the numbers, and places the receiver back on to the cradle. Several times she reaches out for the phone, before withdrawing her hand in mid air. Twice she dials a number, quickly hanging up before the phone has a chance to ring. Taking a deep breath, Diana reaches for the phone again, dialling the number quickly and breathing deeply as she holds the receiver to her ear. The phone rings. Once. Twice. Three times.

"Hello?"

Diana slams the phone back down, her breathing hurried. Picking up the receiver once more, she places it face down on the table and slowly makes her way on to the middle of the bed. Peeling the covers back, Diana slips between the sheets, turns to her side and bends her knees as high as she can. Her eyes heavy, she switches off the light next to the bed and drifts into a restless sleep, alone.

CHAPTER SEVENTEEN

Diana and Dodi sit next to each other in silence as they wait for the midwife to see them. Surprise had registered on Diana's face when she had arrived for the appointment and found Dodi already there, waiting for her. She had not acknowledged him, but sat down next to him and picked up a magazine from the table in front of her. Three members of security had entered the room with her, and aside from Dodi and Diana, they were the only people in the room. Eerily quiet, the sound of the pages of the magazine turning fill the air. The opening of the plain white door in front of them causes both of them to look up and rise simultaneously. The woman standing in front of them is dressed in the standard blue, and has a smiling, friendly face, set upon a large body. Diana's stance immediately relaxes and she smiles at the midwife, before stepping in front of Dodi to offer a greeting and enter the room.

Opening a white folder, the midwife takes out a pen and smiles at the couple seated in front of her

"Hi, I'm Sarah. I don't need to ask either of you your names."

She lets out a high pitched giggle and Diana and Dodi glance at each other, before stifling smiles. The midwife composes herself, and picks up the pen to make some notes

"I know this isn't your first pregnancy, and I have some hospital notes here. Your scan pictures and the notes from your recent inpatient stay in the hospital. Understandable, your blood pressure was a little high last time it was taken, so I'm going to start by taking that if that's ok?"

Sarah gets up slowly, picking up a Velcro cuff with a pump attached to it. Diana rolls up her sleeve in anticipation, focusing on the wall in front of her and breathing deeply as the midwife begins to pump air into the cuff.

"I understand that stress is a very big factor in your life, but for the baby's sake you must try to keep your blood pressure low. High blood pressure can lead to complications such as pre eclampsia which can bring on premature labour."

She looks at the reading on the dial, before struggling back to her seat and writing down the results.

"Your blood pressure is down from the last time it was taken, which is good. Whatever you've been doing, keep at it."

Dodi shoots Diana a smug smile and the air of camaraderie shared between the two moments earlier disappears. The midwife continues

"Right, now I think we're going to have a little listen to the baby's heartbeat and after that we'll have a little sit down and you can talk to me about any worries or concerns that you might have."

She motions Diana to make her way to the table at the back of the room and helps her to clamber up. Shifting slightly to get into a comfortable position, she rests her head back and raises her shirt to expose her slightly rounded stomach. Squeezing a tiny amount of cold gel onto her stomach, Sarah touches Diana's belly with a small white wand and begins moving it in small circles. A few seconds pass before a rhythmic thumping can be heard, echoing slightly through the machinery. The midwife smiles broadly

"That's your baby. The heartbeat sounds perfect."

She leaves the wand in place for several more minutes, allowing the couple to enjoy the sound before switching the machine off and handing Diana a piece of tissue to wipe her stomach.

"I'll give you a few moments to sort yourself out."

Sarah makes her way back to her desk. Wiping the gel off of her stomach, Diana does not look at Dodi, who is staring at her intently. Pulling her top down, she sits up and swings her legs over the edge of the bed, before swaying slightly and letting her head fall forwards. Dodi reaches for her in concern

"What is it? Are you all right?"

Diana smiles weakly

"Dizzy. I just moved too quickly I think."

Dodi takes her arm and helps her down from the bed, supporting most of her weight. When she is steady his grasp lowers enough to take hold of her hand and the two walk back towards the midwifes desk. She smiles

"Well, apart from the slightly high blood pressure, everything looks good, and your blood pressure is coming down so I'm not too worried about that either."

She beams a warm smile at the couple

"Is there anything you wanted to talk to me about? Anything you wanted to ask?"

Diana and Dodi look at each other, before Dodi speaks

"No, I don't think so, thank you."

Diana looks up at the woman in front of her, a concerned look in her eyes

"Obviously we are very concerned about security at the moment. We need to be sure that no details of this, or any future visits, are told to anyone."

Sarah looks mortified

"Of course not. I treat all my patients with the strictest confidences, but your people did make me aware of your special circumstances when they booked you in for this appointment. I can personally guarantee that nothing will go past these four walls, and that, as agreed, I will take no appointments for an hour each side of any that you have to make sure that there is no one else here whilst you are."

Diana looks mollified, and Dodi smiles a grateful smile at the woman in front of them, who relaxes slightly.

"Well if there is nothing else I will see you in two weeks time. I believe you have another scan between now and then?"

Diana nods a confirmation

"Right, well we'll be able to talk about that and keep an eye on your blood pressure at the same time. Any concerns or questions then my numbers are in the pack that was sent out to you."

Diana and Dodi give her their thanks and make their way out into the waiting room where their security team are still stationed. As the couple make their way towards the door, they move in behind them, checking each direction for threats. Diana links her arm through Dodi's and the pair walk out to where their cars are waiting.

Dodi reaches out and takes Diana's hands across the table. She looks down at their entwined fingers before looking back up at him through her eyelashes. Dodi speaks first

"I don't want to cause another fight. All I want to do is explain where I'm coming from to you. Put my point across."

His voice is soft and soothing, but Diana still snatches her hands away and folds them tight across her chest.

"I'm listening."

Her voice is devoid of emotion and her eyes are blank, Dodi's face reflected back in them. He breathes deeply, before beginning.

"I was brought up into Islam. Born a Muslim. It's too much for me to try and sit with you and explain to you because Islam is something that takes a lifetime to learn. It is a path, not a destination. The people at the mosque are family. All my life I've grown up with a support network that consists of hundreds of people. I've had spiritual guidance on tap. How could I not want the same for my child?"

Dodi's hands are outstretched, palms up as if imploring Diana to see his point. She stares back at him indifferently, leaning back in her chair and waiting for him to continue. He begins again.

"Islam stipulates that any child born to a Muslim man should also be brought up as a Muslim. Maybe I didn't go about explaining this to you in the best possible way, but whatever you decide to do I will be taking the baby with me to the mosque when I go. If you decide to remain Christian and take the baby to church with you then that is completely up to you."

"That's not fair Dodi. You know I don't go to church anywhere near as often as you go to the mosque."

Dodi shrugs his shoulders

"You can't use the fact that I'm devoted against me. You could go to church as often as you wanted. Even once a week would be an improvement. Surely a devoted religious upbringing is better than a half arsed one?"

Diana looks as if she is unsure whether she wants to scream or cry. She opens her mouth to speak, but no words come out. Dodi takes advantage of her hesitation to speak again.

"I'm not trying to start an argument Diana, I'm just trying to explain my point. My religion is important to me and it's just as important to me that I share it with my child. I'd like to share it with you too, if you'll let me."

Dodi smiles a warm smile at Diana, who looks confused by the constantly changing tone of the conversation.

"Well, erm, I suppose it won't hurt to look into it more. For me, I mean. I'm not making any promises though."

Dodi beams at Diana and gets out of his seat. He walks around the edge of the table and leans down to hug her tightly. Releasing her, Dodi places a resounding kiss on her lips leaving her looking even more shell shocked than she had previously. Dodi picks up his jacket that had been hanging on the back of the chair.

"I need to pop to work for a few hours, will you be ok by yourself?"

Diana nods once, her eyes slightly glazed over. Dodi leans down and kisses her again, softly this time.

"I'll only be a couple of hours. You're perfectly safe here. The staff will get you anything you need."

Kissing her once more, this time on the top of the head, Dodi walks swiftly to the door and out into the hall. The sound of the front door closing echoes through into the room, leaving Diana alone.

The rooms in Dodi's home are large and ornately decorated, filled with many staff that move about like ghosts. Diana gets up from her perch at the table and begins to walk around the room she has been left in. Although she has been here many times before, she moves slowly, taking time to look at everything as if she is new to the place. A vast bookshelf lines the back wall of the room, dark mahogany shelves filled entirely with leather bound books. Diana runs her fingers over the spines, removing several to leaf through the pages before placing them back where she found them after staring intently at the intricate symbols that fill the pages. Several photographs adorn the room, mostly of Dodi and his family. Diana smiles at seeing both Dodi and his father age as she moves from picture to picture. Having been through the entire room, Diana makes her way to the heavy panelled door and pokes her head out into the corridor. Seeing no one, she slips out of the room and wanders along, smiling at the photographs that continue to line the terracotta walls. Three doors down, Diana finds herself in an almost empty room, save for several prayer mats and copies of the Qur'an. She waits at the door for several moments as if unsure whether to go in, before stepping back out and closing the door behind her. As she turns round to continue on her way, Diana is shocked to find herself almost face to face with one of the usually spirit like staff who see to the running of Dodi's home. She smiles, and tried to step around the man, who holds his ground and stares her firmly in the eye. Black trousers and a white shirt drape on his tiny frame and Diana has easily five inches on him, but something about his stance and demeanour cause her to shrink back from him. He smirks at her, his brown eyes slanted, and begins to carry on along the hallway, Diana flattening herself against the wall to avoid bumping into him. He looks over his shoulder as he begins to descend the stairs, the same smirk still locked on his dark face. Diana waits until he is out of sight, before half running back to the room Dodi had left her in and shutting the door behind her.

CHAPTER EIGHTEEN

He's breathing down the back of my neck and I'm trying hard not to show that it's sending shivers down my spine.

It all started a couple of weeks ago when I went back to the mosque with Jameela. I really wasn't looking forward to it, especially after I got the evil eye off of these two women practically as I walked in the door. It's not unusual for girls to look at me that way, but there was something different about the way these two did it. It wasn't jealousy, you know, the way most girls are. They look at you like you're something that they found on their shoe but deep down you can tell that they're actually desperate to be you. This was different. The women looked at me like I actually was no more than some excrement that they'd have to wipe off of the floor later on. As if my presence was defiling the place that they hold in such high regard. Anyway, I almost turned and walked out but Jameela grabbed hold of my arm and dragged me forwards, grinning at the two women as she went.

It was a youth prayer meeting Jameela had dragged me in for, just a time for people all about the same age to talk about their beliefs and just share experiences about being young and being a Muslim. Everyone there was friendly enough, I was just sitting and listening when this young guy barged through the door, apologising to anyone who would listen. He was tall, way taller than

Matthew, and his skin was a gorgeous caramel colour. He sat opposite me, dumping his bag on the floor and smiled in my direction as everyone carried on with their conversation. Books spilled out from the bag, textbooks by the look of it, so I guessed he was at uni somewhere locally. I was trying to read the titles but I couldn't make them out and when I looked up again he was staring at me with these huge brown and eyes and smiling slightly. I blushed bright red and looked at the floor, but when I looked up he was still staring. My mum always told me that if a boy stares at you for more than five seconds then he's interested and if he stares for more than ten seconds then it's going to be serious. Well, I counted to ten and looked again and he was still staring, smiling pretty widely by that point. After the prayer meeting he came up to introduce himself. Arun, he said his name was. He's a few years older than me and studies religion at one of the universities in central London. He offered to give me a few one on one sessions on Islam, but I told him I had to think about it. It's not wise to let a guy know that you're interested straight off, even if your heart is beating so loud that you're sure he must be able to hear it. That's another thing my mum taught me.

We started private lessons about a week after that. At first he'd just read things out to me and then we'd talk about what I thought it meant and how it made me feel. It's pretty hard to concentrate with those deep, dark eyes gazing at me, but I like to think that I held my own. A lot of the time we didn't agree, still don't, but Arun says that's the point. He thinks that a lot of religious tension in the world is down to people misinterpreting things and that if they just sat down and talked about things then everyone could get along. Because of his studies he can also point out the similarities between Islam and Christianity, show me how a lot of the things that the two religions say are just different sides of the same coin. He told me that Muslims recognise Jesus as a prophet, a bit like Mohammad was, although they dispute that he was the son of God. And Moses too. Arun has a lot of respect for Christianity, it's just a shame, he says, that followers are allowed to be so lax with their worshipping and how sins, over time, have become accepted ways of behaving in Christian society. Like drinking and being promiscuous. My ears got a bit red at that point, because I haven't exactly always been the most chaste of girls, but then he went on to talk about how western girls dress so suggestively and complimented the way that I dress and I forgot all about it. Because of Arun I've become a bit more accepted around the mosque, I've even made some more friends. Last week I even managed to contribute to the prayer meeting, give my opinion on something that was said. I was really pleased that it led on to a whole conversation and afterwards a couple of the people there came over to me to talk about it more and say what a valid point I'd had.

Right now he's trying to talk to me about the pillars of Islam but I can't seem to concentrate today. Arun is wearing that white shirt that sets off his dark complexion perfectly. His hair has been cut so that I can see his dark eyes more clearly and every time he looks at me it's all I can do not to get lost in them. Earlier he brushed against me and I let out a sigh and shivered slightly, prompting him to offer me his jumper, thinking that I was cold. I wasn't, but I took it anyway, wrapping myself up in it. It smells clean and has the slightest hint of something spicy and exotic. I wrap it tighter around me and take a deep sniff from one of the sleeves, before looking up to find Arun staring at me, his nose less than a couple of centimetres from mine.

"Ella, are you ok? You don't seem yourself today."

Oh god he looks seriously concerned and all I can seem to focus on are his lips. They're darker than the rest of his skin, plump and they look really soft. I wonder what it would be like to kiss them. I wonder how he'd feel about me kissing him. After his speech on loose moraled western women I imagine that it wouldn't go down too well. Still, it's nice to dream. His lips are moving again, his hand on my shoulder sending sparks through me.

"Ella, I'm going to get you a glass of water. You just sit there until I get back."

I smile at him, try to tell him that it's not necessary but he's already hurried off. As soon as he's out of the room my head clears a little bit and I stand up and stretch my tired legs. I feel like I've been sitting in the same position for hours, but I really couldn't tell you anything I've learned today. It might be wise to ask for lessons from someone else, but I really can't imagine finding it so enjoyable or being so enthusiastic about learning with anyone else. Arun comes back into the room with a glass of water and a look of concern on his face.

"Ella, I told you to stay sitting down. How are you feeling? You were all over the place for a minute there."

I can feel my face getting hot and I take the glass of water from him and take a mouthful, grateful for the excuse not to have to speak. He's staring at me, waiting for an answer and I hurriedly swallow my mouthful, grimacing as the pain of swallowing too much makes its way down my throat.

"I'm really sorry, I don't seem to have my head on properly today. Thank you for the water though, it's really helped."

Maybe I should tell him that I think someone else should give me lessons. I can't tell him why though. I could use school as an excuse, but he manages and he's further on than I am. I could tell him that I need some time to think about everything, but then he might think I'm wasting his time or that I'm losing interest. In Islam, I mean. Not him. Oh god he's looking at me again.

"Ella?"

And before I know what I'm doing words are rushing out of my mouth

"I'm sorry I'm off today, maybe we could arrange another day this week to talk a bit more. I'm really not taking it in."

He looks stricken and the words keep tumbling out of my mouth

"It's not you, you're a great teacher. Fantastic. You really make it seem all so clear to me. It's just that I've got a lot on with school and stuff and I'm finding it a bit hard to concentrate."

I have no idea where any of that came from, but he looks mollified.

"Well I've got classes a lot of the rest of the week, but if you don't mind meeting me somewhere a bit closer to school maybe we can have a few hours one evening? "

Oh my god, it's like a date. A real date. I can barely keep the grin off of my face.

"That sounds great. Maybe we can get a coffee or something?"

Even I can hear the hope in my voice. I sound so desperate. He's going to see it. He's going to make an excuse and tell me he can't give me lessons any more on account of my desperateness. He smiles warmly

"That sounds great."

I can't stop smiling now. It's one of those smiles that you know is going to make your face hurt, but you're so happy that you don't care. I stand up and start gathering up my notepad and copy of the Qur'an, trying not to let Arun see how happy I am. He's busy gathering up his stuff too. These religion lessons do require a lot of stuff. And time. And effort. I guess that pretty much sums up being a Muslim though. Dedication, I think that's how Arun put it. Dedication and the knowledge that you are living your life in service to Allah. Or something like that. It's really difficult to remember to say Allah instead of God all the time, although to be honest the most I've ever used the word God is in the phrase 'oh my god' and it's not quite the same. I expect if I said 'oh my Allah' it might not have the same connotations, particularly around here.

"So I'll see you Tuesday Ella? Is that ok?"

Oh god (there I go again) I think he's been talking about when and where to meet and I've not been listening. I can't move the blank look off of my face quick enough and he laughs.

"You're really not with it today, are you? I said, there's a little student coffee house just around the corner from my uni, I'll meet you there at about five on Tuesday? Do you know where it is?"

I can't tell him that I looked up where abouts his uni was and when I found out where he was studying I'd memorised which busses I'd need to take. I do my best to look confused.

"I think so. I'm sure I'll find it."

He gives me another one of those heart melting smiles and says goodbye before leaving the room. I wait a minute so I can avoid that awkward moment when you're both going in the same direction for a bit and you say goodbye ten times, before chucking my books into my bag and making my way out. It's going to take a lot of time and effort to plan the perfect outfit for Tuesday. I suppose I should probably do a little bit more studying of the Qur'an too. If I find the time.

Jameela is waiting for me outside, just like she always does, and wants to know about my lesson. We've got pretty close these last few weeks, but in a strange sort of way. All we've got in common is school and Islam, and she seems a lot more into both than I am. Not that I'm not into them, it's just I have other things I like to think about too. I tried talking to Jameela about her love life the other day and she just clammed right up. I don't know if that's a religious thing or just a personal one. It's not really something I can ask her either, or Arun for that matter. Not without making it sound like I'm trying to suss out how he feels about me. It's all very complicated, but Diana seems to be making it look so easy.

CHAPTER NINETEEN

"It's not easy, you know!"

Diana's voice is high pitched as she flings the newspaper down on the table. Once again her face adorns the front cover, speculation about her conversion filling the pages. Dodi looks up at Diana, his face a mixture of amusement and confusion.

"What's not easy?"

Diana stops pacing around the table and stares at him

"Reading about this day in and day out. Having the world questioning me and my motives. Will she, won't she?"

Dodi sighs deeply

"It's not like you're not used to having your life constantly written and talked about, but if it bothers you that much then make a decision and then you can set the record straight."

Diana places her hands over her ever expanding bump and stares coldly at Dodi

"And how exactly am I supposed to do that? It's not a decision you make over night."

Diana reaches back towards the paper she has discarded on the table and leafs through it until she finds what she is looking for. Printed practically in the centre of the page is an open letter to Dodi, listing the many reasons why Diana is not a good example of what a Muslim woman should be and urging him to end their relationship.

"And from the looks of it the decision isn't exactly in my hands anyway."

Dodi groans audibly and reaches out to take Diana's hand, but she snatches it away.

"I was hoping that you wouldn't see that. It's just a one off letter from a crazy fanatic. You shouldn't listen to anything written in there."

Dodi tries to grab the paper from Diana, but she snatches it out of his grasp.

"So I should just ignore where he's written that I could *never be as chaste or as pure as an Islamic woman is required to be*? Or the bit that goes on to say *Diana is too westernised, too opinionated and outspoken to be the sort of wife a Muslim man deserves*? Come on Dodi, the paper wouldn't have printed this if they didn't at least think it would provoke some sort of reaction, or they hadn't had several letters in a similar vein."

Dodi pulls a chair out from underneath the table and sinks into it with an air of defeat.

"There are always going to be people unhappy with a woman like you marrying a man like me. It could be for many different reasons, but this time it just happens to be about religion. It could have been about skin colour or politics. You can't please all of the people all of the time Diana, as long as you and I are happy nothing else really matters, does it?"

Diana positions herself at the opposite side of the table and pulls the chair out. She sits down slowly and draws the chair in as much as her protruding stomach will allow her. Dodi continues

"Think about the welcome you've been given on your visits to the mosque. How many times have you been now? Two? Three?"

Diana nods once

"They've been thrilled about you coming to learn about Islam, you said to me yourself that you couldn't have felt more welcome. Just as many, if not more, people would be thrilled that such a high profile and well respected woman would turn to Islam. If that was what you decided, obviously."

Dodi hurriedly tacks the last sentence on, in response to the look on Diana's face. Angry a moment ago, Diana now looks as if she might cry

"Are you sure that you don't think those things about me? That I'm not the right sort of woman?"

Dodi gets up and walks around the table, pulling Diana's chair out and sinking to his knees before wrapping his arms around her

"Of course I don't think that. Diana, I asked you to marry me because as far as I'm concerned you are perfect. The perfect woman in every sense. I won't deny that if you were to convert to Islam it would make me the happiest man in the world, because we would be sharing something so special. But whatever your decision, you are still perfect to me. Muslim or otherwise."

Diana considers his words for a moment

"They have been very welcoming at the mosque, really considerate too. Do you think that's just because my conversion might bring more people to Islam?"

Dodi opens his mouth, before thinking better of whatever he was about to say and closing it again. When he does speak it is clear that he has chosen his words carefully.

"You know how when you go out wearing something the next day the shops are full of that exact same style?"

Diana looks confused, but nods once and waits for him to continue

"Women like to wear what you wear, and in the same way, women like to do what you do. I have no doubt that some women will start to look into Islam simply because they think that's what you're doing. Some of these women will see it as something fashionable, nothing more than a fad. However it is still a good opportunity to bring Islam into the western world, to spread the word even further. Even one more person put on the right path is something to be grateful for. I am sure that the idea that people will follow you into Islam has crossed the minds of the people at the mosque, but honestly, I think they would be just as thrilled to have you if you were just some woman who had strolled in off of the street in search of knowledge."

Diana smiles a small smile and looks down at Dodi, still on his knees in front of her. She leans forward, slightly hampered by her stomach, and kisses him softly on the lips. Dodi grins at her and begins to pull himself back up into a standing position. Still holding Diana's hand, he leans down and kisses it, before smiling widely at her.

"I've got to go to work, but I think my father will be popping in for coffee soon. And the boys will be round after school."

Diana smiles widely at hearing this, her blue eyes lighting up at the mention of her sons

"Until then you're to keep resting, like the midwife said."

Diana drops her hands to her sides in frustration

"I can't stay on bed rest for the entire pregnancy. I'll go mad!"

"I know it's frustrating. How about we see what your blood pressure is like at the next midwife appointment and go from there."

Diana raises her eyebrow at Dodi

"If it's gone down then I can start doing things again? Maybe like picking the boys up from school?"

Dodi sighs and looks Diana in the eye

"You know that both the police and our security teams have advised us against doing anything we would normally do. That's why I have to take a different route to work every time I go and do as much as I can from home. Picking the boys up is just asking for trouble Diana. How would you feel if something happened in front of them? Or god forbid, to them?"

Diana sighs softly but before she can speak Dodi begins again

"And every time we leave the house you're terrified anyway. The last time we were in the car together you held on to my hand like you were afraid you were going to fall out. And don't even get me started on the ridiculous disguises."

Diana looks insulted and struggles to her feet, nudging Dodi with her shoulder as she passes him and muttering
    "Hadn't you better be getting off to work?"

As she leaves the room. Dodi throws his hands in the air in frustration and follows her out of the door.
    Diana waits for the sound of the front door slamming before slumping down in the armchair and switching the TV on. Her gaze wanders around the room as she waits for the set to load, before using the remote to scan through the channels. On her third flick through she settles on the news, turning sideways and flinging her legs over the arm of the sofa in an attempt to make herself comfortable. Struggling to lean forwards, Diana props a cushion behind her back and rests both of her hands on her small bump. Her eyes are just beginning to close when the sound of her own name causes her to open her eyes and struggle back into a sitting position. On the news, a woman with big hair and too much make up is talking about demonstrations and protests in several cities around England. On a screen behind her, a picture of Diana and Dodi is displayed, Dodi's hand resting lovingly on Diana's stomach while she smiles up at him. The woman stops talking and the photograph merges into a video of people marching through a town centre. Men and women, of all ages, are holding placards and banners and chanting. They march right past the

camera, several people looking directly at it with a meaningful look in their eyes. The sound on the TV set is low and Diana turns up the volume, leaning forward so she can hear their words more clearly.

"Islam is not a fad. Reject the western interlopers."

Primarily Asian, there are several hundred people gathered. Some of them clutch copies of the Qur'an and the majority of the women wear the traditional burka, covering them in their entirety, except for their eyes. The camera pans for several moments, to show the audience just how vast the crowd that has assembled is, before turning to the journalist leading the story. She is standing with a middle aged Asian man, one of the ones who is clutching a copy of the Qur'an. Clearly this is the later part of the interview as she doesn't bother to introduce him, but leads in straight with a question.

"You said earlier that this protest is about keeping Islam pure. Can you elaborate a bit more on what you mean by this?"

The man takes a deep breath, before looking at the camera and speaking in perfect but heavily accented English

"Islam seems to have become something of a focus for the British media recently, there has been a lot written in the papers about Dodi Al Fayed and Diana. That a Muslim man would begin a relationship with such a woman, let alone get her pregnant is something completely unheard of, a lot of the Muslim community were quite distressed by this."

The anchor interrupts him at this point

"I can understand that their relationship could seem a little unorthodox, but then surely the fact that she is considering converting to Islam could only be a good thing?"

"People might see it that way, but Islam is a very serious religious commitment. It is not something that should be undertaken on a whim."

"There is no indication that this is a whim on Diana's part. Perhaps she is looking for a more fulfilling, spiritual life."

The man smiles a condescending smile at the woman who is interviewing him

"I think we all know Diana doesn't do serious commitment."

Diana hurls the remote at the TV, the corner catching the power button and plunging the screen into darkness

"Small minded, bigoted arsehole."

Diana screams the words before collapsing back in a heap on the sofa, tears streaming down her face. A small cough from the corner of the room, announces the presence of a witness to Diana's breakdown and as she looks up Mohammad Al Fayed enters the room, his face a mask of concern.

CHAPTER TWENTY

Mohammad Al Fayed leans over Diana, a steaming cup of coffee in one hand. Diana, stretched out on the sofa, has closed her eyes, her chest rising and falling slowly. With his free hand, Mohammad reaches out and gently touches her shoulder, causing Diana to jerk awake violently and the coffee to slosh down the side of the cup and on to the sofa.

"God, I'm so sorry. You startled me."

Diana struggles to sit up and takes the offered cup and places it on the table before rising and making her way to the door, before his voice calls her back

"Leave it, there isn't much mess. The staff will deal with it later."

Diana turns and makes her way back to the sofa somewhat reluctantly, her face still tearstained from her earlier tantrum. She lowers herself somewhat clumsily back down on to the sofa, smiling at her future father in law. He returns the smile and gestures at the cup of coffee sitting on the table.

"I thought it might help. Coffee always makes me feel better when I'm having a bad day."

His words are kind, the tone inviting confidences. Diana looks torn for a moment, before speaking

"Have you seen the news today?"

Mohammad Al Fayed snorts loudly
    "Morons, all of them. They haven't a clue what they're talking about. I wouldn't worry about it my dear."

He pats Diana on the arm in a gesture that is clearly meant to be reassuring. Diana looks into his deep brown eyes, so similar to those of his sons, and seems to search them for any trace that he could be keeping things from her.
    "They certainly had a lot to say on the matter. And there were so many of them, so many people willing to protest against me."

Diana looks hurt, her fair features a picture of sadness.
    "There are always people who aren't happy about something. Always people who think that they know best. I, personally, have spoken to many people who agree that Dodi is happier than he has ever been and that the two of you are wonderful together."

Diana smiles softly at this, before her expression turns sour again
    "What about all the things they said about me converting to Islam? That I'm not the right sort of woman? That I'm not good enough."

Mohammad snorts again and utters a few words in a language Diana doesn't understand, before addressing her in English
    "There is no right or wrong type of person as far as Islam is concerned. As long as a person is dedicated to

the path and a true believer then anyone is welcome. All Muslims should be grateful for every single person that converts, because that is one more person who has become enlightened to the teaching of the Prophet Mohammad, peace be upon him."

Before Diana can respond to this he begins again

"Dodi told me you had been going to the mosque, Diana. I can't tell you how happy this makes me."

Diana smiles weakly and leans forwards to pick up the coffee cup from the table and wraps her hands around it, focusing intently on her own interlocking fingers. When she doesn't respond he begins again

"I know you're going to get so much out of your visits there. Dodi is so excited to be sharing this with you, and the baby too, of course."

Diana is still staring intently at her coffee, having yet to take a sip.

"We haven't decided yet what religion the baby will be."

Diana raises her coffee to her lips and takes a long swig, glancing sideways to see how Mohammad has reacted to the news. His mouth opens and closes several times before he manages to form a complete sentence

"But of course the baby will be Muslim. The baby is always a Muslim. Dodi told me you had spoken about this."

Diana puts the coffee cup down and looks him straight in the eye

"We have talked about it. And we decided that Dodi could take the baby to the mosque if he wishes, but also that if I want to take the baby to church I will do."

For a moment Mohammad looks stunned, as if Diana had slapped him. He stares at her wordlessly for a few moments before spluttering

"I was under the impression that your conversion was imminent, at least, that was how Dodi made it sound."

Diana made a most unladylike sound, before folding her hands across her bump in a gesture that appears almost defensive

"I bet he did. Well, no decisions have been made about that, either."

Her tone is sharp and once she finishes speaking she purses her lips into a thin line. Mohammad stares at her for a few seconds, taking in the look on her face and her defensive body language.

"I'm sorry, it may have been a misunderstanding on my part. I did not mean to imply that Dodi had told me anything, only that I had made a presumption. Which was clearly wrong."

Diana does not relax her posture, but concedes

"Yes, you were. I'll make sure you are correctly informed if and when any real decisions are made."

The pair sit in silence for a while, neither of them looking at the other. After a couple of minutes, Mohammad tries again

"Are you planning on visiting the mosque again?"

His tone is cautious, as if he is afraid of offending her, or speaking out of turn. Diana still does not look at him as she responds.

"It was my intention, yes, but after watching the news today and seeing what was written in the papers, I am not sure."

"Please at least take the time to discuss what you have seen and read with the mosque you have been going to. I am sure they will have a unique insight into it, and a completely opposite opinion to offer."

His tone is imploring, hands held out in front of him. Diana shrugs noncommittally.

"I'm practically on house arrest at the moment. I can't see how I'd manage to go, even if I wanted to."

Mohammad smiles widely

"That is not a problem. I will arrange a home visit. Yes, in the interest of yours and the baby's safety and security, a home visit would be much wiser. I will speak to Dodi and find out a time that is convenient for the both of you. The Imam at the mosque I attend, the same one that Dodi went to when he was younger, is an old friend of mine, always keen to welcome new converts into the fold. I am sure that he would be delighted to have a personal hand in your spiritual enlightenment."

Diana opens her mouth to speak, but no words come out. Her jaw hangs slack for several seconds before she slams her mouth shut and purses her lips back into a thin, tight line. Mohammad Al Fayed seemingly takes her silence as acceptance of her plan, as he rises and begins making his way towards the door, muttering to himself.

"I will make the phone call right away, I'm sure he will be delighted to hear of this."

And then in a louder tone
"Thank you for your hospitality my dear."

He rushes back to kiss Diana softly on both cheeks, cupping her face gently in his hands and examining her
"No, don't get up. I am perfectly capable of seeing myself to the door. Anyway, from the looks of it you need all the rest you can get."

Diana who has begun to raise herself out of her chair, slumps back down most ungracefully. She barely waits for Mohammad to leave before closing her eyes. A single tear slips from her eyes once the sound of the front door closing reaches up to her. Wiping the tear away, Diana shifts herself back into the position she had been in previously, her legs swung over the arm of the chair. She props a cushion behind her head and settles both hands on her bump as she begins to drift off into an exhausted sleep.

It is clear from her confused expression that Diana is not immediately sure where she is when she awakens. The room is dark but the TV glows softly in the corner of the room. A young, male voice fills the air
"Harry, I said you could watch the television once you were finished with your homework."

Diana smiles widely and struggles into a sitting position. William and Harry rush to her side.
"Mother, are you all right? Is there anything we can get for you?"

Williams face is a picture of concern, his forehead creased up towards his sandy hair. Harry takes his mother's hand and smiles up at her angelically. Diana lets go of his hand and draws both boys close to her in a warm embrace

"I'm fine, I was just resting. I'm so sorry I was asleep when you got here. Are you both OK? Did you have a good day at school?"

Diana leans back from her boys to examine their faces, before drawing each boy close once again and planting kisses on their foreheads. Harry rubs the spot with the cuff of his blazer, prompting a laugh from his mother and brother. William speaks

"Harry has homework to do. I've done mine."

Harry aims a dirty look at his brother before heading back to the table where his books are laid out. William moves to sit next to his mother, who shuffles over on the chair and the pair of them squeeze into the single seat. William rests his hand on his mothers round stomach affectionately.

"Do you know if it's a boy or a girl?"

Diana shakes her head.

"I'd quite like a sister. It would be nice to have a little girl around. Harry and I could take care of her."

Diana looks at the thoughtful expression on her sons face and laughs softly before wrapping her arm around him and pulling him close for a hug. When William breaks free from his mothers embrace he has a troubled look on his face

"What's wrong?"

Diana is concerned as William seems unable to vocalise what is on his mind. When he does speak, his four words explain his expression

"I've seen the news."

Diana's face changes from an expression of mild confusion to one of concern. She tries to cover it quickly by smiling widely and responding in an overly bright tone

"You can't please all of the people all of the time. Some people just like to have something to moan about."

Diana struggles out of the chair she is sharing with her son and makes her way towards the television, keeping her back to William.

"It's still not nice to hear. Especially with everything else that is going on."

William does not acknowledge the attempt on his mother's life, but it hangs unspoken in the air. Diana turns to stare at her son, examining his youthful face. She returns back to her chair, wedging herself in against him and slipping her arm across his shoulders

"For such a young man, you are very wise. Wise enough to know, that with all the blessings we have been given in this life, sometimes we must also face the negative side of living such a public life."

William nods gravely and reaches across Diana's stomach to take her free hand, before looking up at her with a solemn expression on his face.

"Are you happy?"

His tone is soft, his blue eyes bright and keen.

Diana nods once, before practically whispering
  "Yes. I'm very happy."

William either does not see, or pretends not to, her blue eyes filling with tears. He kisses her gently on the cheek before leaping out of the seat and heading towards where his brother is seated. Diana watches as William leans over Harry's homework and points something out to his younger brother. The two boys laugh together as silent tears slip unnoticed down their mother's cheeks.

Chapter Twenty One

I can see him waiting for me, right there in the cafe. I know I'm late and I really should go in but I can't help hanging around to look at him a bit longer. He's so gorgeous! There are a couple of girls in there who are queuing for coffee and giving him the eye, but he's so engrossed in whatever he's looking at that he doesn't notice. He looks at his watch though, which tells me I'd better get a move on. Plus it'll be nice to sit down with him after those cheap looking girls have been practically dribbling all over him. I open the door and the warm air hits me, causing me to shiver once and sending a tingling through my freezing arms and legs. I hurry towards the table, pulling off my gloves and scarf as I move.

"Arun?"

He looks up at me with those gorgeous brown eyes

"I'm so sorry I'm late, I got completely lost and then someone gave me the wrong directions"

He's smiling up at me and I feel a little bit guilty for lying to him, especially as we're technically supposed to be meeting to talk about Islam and Allah. Still, what he doesn't know won't hurt him, and he really doesn't need to know just how long it took to pick out the perfect outfit.

"It's not a problem Ella. Actually I was glad of five minutes to myself to look over some things."

He stands up and pulls my chair out and for a second I feel like a princess. I wonder if that was one of the things that Diana likes about Dodi, that he makes her feel like a princess again. It must be pretty hard to go from being a fairytale princess to suddenly not being one anymore. Arun is speaking to me and I seem to have missed it again. I really should make a conscious effort to concentrate around him

"Ella? I asked if you had a good week."

I blush and nod, not trusting that my mouth won't open up and spill something that it's not supposed to. It's happened before.

"Good. Well then I think we should make a start where we left off, don't you? How much do you remember about the pillars of Islam?"

Ok, so I meant to do some studying this week, I really did. It's just that I then started worrying about what I was going to wear and how I was going to act and the week just disappeared. I figure the only way out of this is to be honest. Anyway, the less I claim to know the longer these sessions have to go on.

"Not a lot."

I try to look embarrassed, but he still looks a bit annoyed. Oh god, what if he decides I'm too stupid to teach? What if my lack of dedication makes him think that I'm one of the hangers on that those people on the news have been talking about? Just following a trend? Getting into Islam because it's fashionable?

"I'm really sorry, it's just that last session, I had so much on my mind. And I really tried to look at it this week, but it just makes so much more sense when you explain it to me."

My eyes are filling up with tears and Arun shifts in his seat and looks uncomfortable. Good, he's falling for it. If he can just let me get away with being a bit lapse this one time then I promise I'll be a better student. I couldn't cope with not getting to see him anymore. He breathes in and out a few times before speaking in that gorgeous deep voice of his

"Ok, let's go through this again then."

It was a depressingly boring session. There was this one time that I thought Arun was playing footsie with me under the table but it turns out it was just this girls bag from the table over that I was rubbing against. She didn't look too pleased about that. But apart from that it was all Islam and the prophet Mohammad (peace be upon him.)That's not to say that it's not interesting, because it is, but I still can't help but hope for a little bit more. Still there was one promising development. Arun noticed how much better I was concentrating and decided that we should have all our sessions there from now on, as long as I didn't mind. It's fine by me, because that means I get to see him at the mosque and outside as well. Not that I told him this. I just agreed that it was easier for me to get my head around things in a less formal situation. No need to tell him how much effort went in to concentrating that hard.

I switch on the TV as soon as I get in and try to fill my mind with something a bit less meaningful and profound. It's not that I don't appreciate meaningful and profound, but between Islam and my classes sometimes it's nice to just switch off for a while. I kick off my shoes, swing my leg over the arm of the sofa and pick up the remote to have a bit of a flick through what's on. On the first channel the news is on and a picture of Diana fills the main screen. It's the shot of her and Dodi when they first announced their pregnancy and Diana looks particularly lovely. Pregnancy really suits her. Well, at least when she's not afraid for her life. The woman on the news chatters on for a bit before the screen flicks to a shot of a city centre filled with people. Another protest. God, it's unbelievable. I mean, the people at the mosque Jameela took me to couldn't have been more understanding about me being there, and helpful too. Poor Diana only wants to look into the religion that is such a big part of her future husbands life and people are actively campaigning against it. You'd have to have pretty thick skin for something like that not to bother you, especially at such an emotional point in her life. I bet she's in pieces, bless her.

I had to change the channel. All I kept thinking about was how poor Diana must be feeling and I found myself getting quite angry. Some people are so closed minded, so arrogant. You'd think that they'd be pleased to have someone with such a big profile drawing attention to their way of life. How dare they think that Islam is only for certain people, only for the right sort of people? Arun has been teaching me about how for thousands of years Muslims have been fighting to defend their way of life, to try to bring understanding to the rest of the world. And we've spent ages looking at the similarities between Christianity and Islam. Fair enough, I know Diana hasn't always been the most morally upright person, the best example of a Christian, but who has? She's been through so much, and everyone knows what a good person she is. Look at all the charity work she does. And how much she loves her children. God, I was getting so annoyed just thinking about it. And then I couldn't help thinking about me and how these sort of people must feel about me getting into Islam. I mean, I haven't exactly been the best Christian either. I've been out drinking, I've slept with a few guys and I hardly ever do so much as buy the Big Issue. I tell myself that it's because I'm a student and I need to save every penny, but really it's just because I'm not that nice. If Diana, after spending all that time working with people with AIDS and all the stuff she does for that anti landmine charity, isn't the right sort of person to become a Muslim, that where does that leave me? Or the rest of people who might be interested in converting? If they look at the news they'll think 'these people don't want Diana so they're certainly not going to want me."

I called Arun. He'd given me his phone number in case I wanted to talk about anything and I'd got myself so worked up I just had to call. His Dad had answered and had been really friendly, but I could hear his Mum muttering something in the background that I couldn't understand. Can't blame her though really. When I lived at home my Mum always had something to say when a boy called. When Arun came to the phone he sounded quite concerned. Even through my practical hysterics I couldn't help but be pleased that he seemed worried about me.

"Ella, is everything ok?"

I managed to hiccough through my story; that I'd seen the news and how some of the Muslim community felt about Diana and where did that leave me and was I really the right sort of person to convert to Islam, did everyone secretly feel like I wasn't good enough, wasn't moral enough. I'd got myself into quite a state by this point, and bless him, he just sat and listened patiently, waiting for me to calm down before saying

"I'm on my way over."

So now I'm waiting for him to turn up. I pretty much forgot all about my hysterics when he said that he was coming and just got really excited. I was halfway through sorting out the mess I'd made of my make up before I remembered that I'm supposed to be upset. I put on the TV and tuned back into the news to calm me down a bit. Still, I had to make sure I didn't look a complete mess when I went to open the door. As soon as I buzzed him up I went to the bathroom and stuck a bit of concealer under my eyes and ran a brush through my hair. It's hard not to run to the door once I hear him knock, but I manage to take my time, opening it slowly as if I'm not sure who is there. As soon as the door is open wide enough Arun charges through and wraps his arms around me, pulling me into a tight embrace. I'm trying to relax and enjoy the moment but my heart is pounding away and my head is very conscious of the fact that we've never been this close before. When he breaks away he looks embarrassed and looks at the floor as he speaks

"I'm really sorry. I didn't mean to just barge in and do that, it's just you sounded so upset on the phone."

He looks up at me, his head still hanging low and a faint blush on his cheeks. I can't help but smile at the look on his face.

"Don't worry about it. I think I was overreacting anyway. I mean, the stuff on the news is quite distressing but everyone has been so nice to me so far."

I gesture my arm out as I'm talking and Arun makes his way through into the tiny living area in my little student flat. I'd had a bit of a tidy up when he said he was coming, and left all the books he'd given me open on the little table to make it look like I'd been studying. I would have been too, if it wasn't for all that stuff on the news upsetting me. Arun seems pleased to see it though, he smiles widely at me as I sit down next to him on the cramped sofa. He gestures to the books.

"I see you've been studying. Now I'm here did you want to look over anything, or talk about anything with me?"

I turn to look at him to answer and find him staring at me. Our noses are practically touching and those big brown eyes are boring into me. My heart starts beating at a million miles an hour and I can hardly think, definitely can't speak. He hasn't moved, I think he's waiting for me to say something but it's all I can do to keep breathing in and out. I can't kiss him, after everything he's said and everything on the news about western women. I can't, but I want to so badly. And then it doesn't matter because his lips are on mine and he's kissing me and it doesn't matter that I can't think and I can't breathe. Every thought, fear, concern and worry has flown right out of my head. Because he's kissing me and everything is perfect.

CHAPTER TWENTY TWO

Diana stares into the mirror forlornly, before turning sideways to examine her now football like bump. She seemed to have exploded into pregnancy over the last few weeks, most of her clothes no longer fitting comfortably. She sighs and places her hands over the bump, smiling as the baby visibly shifts inside of her. Stepping away from the mirror, Diana reaches out to the telephone on her bedside table and picks up the receiver.

"I need the car and driver please, as soon as possible."

Leaving her room, Diana stops only to pick up her wig, glasses and scarf, before exiting her front door and waiting on the steps for the car to arrive. It isn't long before the now standard black four by four pulls up outside the house and a smartly dressed young man hurries round to open the door for her. Diana beams at him

"Thank you."

And steps into the car. Strapping herself in firmly, she grips hold of the seat and leans across to peer in the rear view mirror to make sure her disguise is flawless. The driver, breathing heavily from hurrying back to his seat asks

"Where to Ma'am?"

"Central London please. I need to do some shopping."

The driver nods once and puts the car into gear, moving slowly down the driveway. Diana leans back in her seat, hand still firmly gripped in place, and stares out of the window. The heavy tint on the glass means that it is impossible to see inside of the car, a recent addition which Diana had insisted on. Press no longer adorn the edge of her property, clearly fed up with seeing so little of her over the last few months. Diana smiles when she sees no one waiting to pounce with a camera and relaxes further into the back of the seat. Once they are a fair distance from her home she leans forward and cranks the window open slightly, closing her eyes and letting the breeze fall onto her face. She has practically dozed off when the driver stops the car and announces

"Oxford Street, Ma'am. Would you like me to wait for you?"

Diana leans forward to check her disguise in the mirror again before responding

"I think I am going to be a while, but I may need you in a hurry so it would probably be best if you were to stay somewhere convenient."

She does not wait for him to come round and open the door, instead exiting alone and slamming the door behind her as she hurries towards the shops. Having slipped out without her security team, Diana moves about cautiously, almost like a child afraid of being caught playing truant. Her face slowly morphs into a smile as she loses herself in the sea of people milling up and down the road, no one stopping long enough to look at her properly, everyone too wrapped up in their own business to bother to look past her disguise.

Diana takes her time, walking slowing and stopping to look in several shop windows before actually entering any of the stores. She stands entranced for a good ten minutes at a nursery display set up in one of the windows. Several passersby bump into her and mutter angry words in her direction before she makes her way towards the front of the store. Ignoring the basket offered to her by a bored looking member of staff, Diana heads to the escalator and begins the slow ascent to the second floor, where a shiny sign proclaims the maternity section is located. Struggling to pull her coat around her, Diana checks her wig and sunglasses in a mirror before entering the department and begins to nose around at the tiny clothes. Another shop assistant makes their way over, offering a wicker basket and their personal shopping service. Diana shakes her head softly, offering a small smile to excuse the fact that she doesn't vocalise her response, taking the wicker basket and turning away before the young woman can press her further.

The department is practically empty, just a few other expectant mothers wondering around, writing the names of things down on the stores luxury headed paper. Diana avoids these women as much as possible, keeping herself to herself and piling her little wicker basket high with small white clothes and tiny fluffy blankets. Twice she catches her image in one of the store mirrors and seems surprised to find that her reflection is smiling. Diana moves towards the furniture displays laid out in the middle of the floor and runs her hand longingly across the smooth finish of an intricate mahogany crib, smiling as it begins to swing slightly at her touch. Helping herself to a piece of the stationary laid out conveniently next to the display and one of the stores monogrammed ballpoint pens, Diana notes down the item number of the crib. Clutching her basket tightly, she moves towards the rest of the display, quickly noting down the item numbers for the matching cot, wardrobe, chest of drawers and changing unit. Her smile now spread across her whole face, Diana makes her way towards the check out and the young woman she had been so surly towards

"I'd like another basket please. And could you keep hold of this one whilst I finish my shopping please?"

Diana smiles sweetly at the woman who accepts the proffered basket and exchanges it for an empty one, all the time staring strangely at the woman in front of her. Diana beams

"Thank you so much."

Before heading towards the maternity clothing section.

By the time Diana has finished her shopping, her two baskets are piled high with clothes of all sizes and her list of items requiring delivery at a later date fills almost an entire A4 page. The young girl at the till stares at her, mouth agape, not even bothering to try to hide her amazement. Diana hums to herself, barely noticing as her things are scanned through at a snail's pace. When the total is announced, Diana does not balk at the monstrous amount, but simply hands over her small, golden piece of plastic. Without looking at the name on the card, the girl swipes it through the till and hands Diana the small receipt, waiting for her to sign her name. As soon as she hands back the small slip of paper and pen, the girl pushes a delivery slip to her and indicates where Diana needs to fill in her information. Diana waits patiently for the girl to hand her back the pen

"These items will be with you within fourteen days at no cost to you. If you wanted them sooner than that..."

The girl eyes Diana's stomach
"Then it will be at a charge of five pounds."

Diana smiles widely and pushes the paper and pen back to the girl
"No, fourteen days sounds absolutely perfect. Is there someone who can help me to my car with the rest of these bags?"

The girl does not respond. Instead she is staring, mouth open once again, at the piece of paper Diana has handed her. Diana waits for a moment, before prompting
"Excuse me....?"

The girls head snaps up at the sound of Diana's distinctive voice, her eyes squinting at the woman in front of her as if to try and see through her dark glasses. When she speaks her voice is loud and carries across the store
"You're......"

Diana shakes her head vigorously at the girl and looks over both her shoulders, before motioning her to be quiet.
"Princess Diana."

Several heads across the store snap up, the other women scattered across the maternity department all begin to make their way discreetly towards the till. Diana looks back over her shoulders in a panic.

"No, I'm not."

Her voice is forceful and there is a harsh, warning edge to her tone. The girl behind the till blushes scarlet.

"S-s-sorry, I must have been mistaken."

Her apology is nowhere near as loud as her earlier assertion and does nothing to stop the women around the store from beginning to crowd around the till. Although there are no more than five of them and they all stand a good metre away from Diana, her face begins to take on the look of a frightened animal and her breaths are short and laboured. The women mutter around her

"Look at all the stuff she's bought."

"Didn't realise it was her. Saw her looking at something pink earlier. She must be having a girl."

"I wonder if we've bought any of the same things?"

"You wait till I tell my husband."

Diana's gaze flashes back and forth from the store assistant and the women gathered around her, before reaching towards her bags on the till and gathering them all up in her arms. Barely able to see, she pushes past the women and heads towards the escalator, her breathing becoming more laboured with every step.

Diana bursts out of the main door way and into the bustle of Oxford Street, her arms still filled with bags of shopping. Several shoppers are forced to swerve to avoid hitting her as she stands in the middle of the street motionless. Inside the shop the sales assistant hurries down the escalator, waving a forgotten item in the air and calling loudly after her fleeing customer. Seemingly refusing to learn from her earlier faux pas, she calls out

Diana's name loudly in a bid to get her attention. As the sound drifts from the doorway people slow down and begin muttering to each other

"She said Princess Diana."

"I'm sure she was calling for Diana. Do you think she means THE Diana?" Where?"

Foot traffic comes to an almost complete standstill as people begin to search around, clearly looking for a tall, blonde, heavily pregnant woman. Diana, her hair and face still covered, and bags of clothes obscuring the view of her stomach, remains unnoticed. As the sound of her name draws closer, Diana begins to push her way past people, items of clothing spilling from the heavily loaded bags in her arms. The murmurs from people querying Diana's location soon turn into complaints as, unbeknown to them, she shoves past. Moving slowly because of her heavy load and the sheer amount of people, Diana is soon caught by the young shop assistant, who has been gathering up the rest of the items that Diana has dropped.

"Princess Diana! You forgot this."

The girl places an item on top of the large pile Diana is struggling with

"And this. And this. And this."

The girl smiles and looks pleased with herself as she adds each item to the stack, not noticing Diana is already struggling. The people around are staring, whispering to each other and it seems as if the whole of Oxford Street has come to a standstill to gawk at Diana. Her cheeks flushed, Diana's wig has been knocked sideways and half of her matted blonde hair is visible. The tearstains that streak her cheeks from underneath her dark glasses and her armful of shopping spilling endlessly give her the look of someone on the verge of a breakdown. Clearly someone in the shop has alerted the press, as photographers appear as if from nowhere and begin clicking incessantly. Frozen to the spot, Diana does not move as they descend on her, drawing ever closer and shouting questions in her direction. In sympathy to her plight, the shoppers form a wall around Diana and draw in tighter, keeping the photographers at a safe distance as the public shouts at them to leave her alone. Diana, remains frozen in her protective circle, shaking and waiting as one of the members of the public hails her a taxi. Several women help Diana into the cab, bundling all of her purchases in with her and instructing the driver to take her home, before slamming the door. As the taxi pulls away the photographers chase after her, cameras flashing in the hope of getting a photograph of Diana falling apart.

Chapter Twenty Three

Dodi slams the door on his way in, causing Diana to flinch even from her chair in the sitting room. He storms into the room, his face crumpled up in anger

"Are you absolutely insane?"

Diana cringes at the volume of his voice and replies meekly

"Do we have to talk about this now? I've had a hard enough day."

"Of course you've had a hard day. For some reason, completely unknown to me, you seemed to think it was a good idea to just disappear out of the house today. Without your security team!"

Dodi's voice rises even louder with the last four words and Diana sinks even lower into her chair. He continues to shout, seemingly unaware of the effect he is having on her.

"And then I find out that it was all so you could go shopping! Shopping? Diana!"

Diana's face turns defensive.

"I'm sick of being on house arrest. And if you hadn't noticed, none of my clothes fit properly anymore. *And* we haven't bought anything for the baby and my due date is getting ever closer."

Dodi slumps down into the easy chair opposite Diana and places his hand across his forehead, a thumb and finger on each temple.

"And you didn't think of looking in a catalogue? Sending one of your assistants?"

Diana pouts

"It's not the same. The things in catalogues are never the same as they are in the pictures, and I can't trust someone else to pick out clothes for me, and I want to be the one picking out clothes for my child."

Dodi looks up at her

"Our child. Don't you think I might have liked to be involved in that too?"

Diana looks abashed as he continues

"But you didn't even think to wait for me. Or even the security team, after everything we've been through. What the hell were you thinking?"

Dodi pushes himself out of the chair and begins to pace around the room as Diana replies

"I wasn't thinking I suppose. It was a bit of an impulse and I'm sorry, but don't you think I've been punished enough?"

Dodi stares at her coldly.

"You think that I'm going to feel sorry for you because you went out into the middle of central London by yourself and someone recognised you? You've been telling me for weeks that you don't want to come to the mosque with me because you're afraid of being photographed and what the papers will say, and then you disappear shopping and end up being caught by photographers having some sort of breakdown on Oxford Street. What do you think the papers are going to say tomorrow?"

Diana doesn't meet his gaze, instead wrapping her hands across her stomach and looking at the floor.

"And then my father arranges for someone to come and talk to you about Islam, take time out of their schedule as a personal favour, and you turn them away?"

Diana's looks up at Dodi, her eyes cold

"I. Had. A. Headache."

She enunciates each word carefully as if she has said them many times before.

"And how did this become yet another conversation about religion? I'm really getting sick of hearing it Dodi."

Diana raises her voice slightly, a cold hard edge to her tone.

"I'm sorry about today. I was wrong, and I've admitted that and I've apologised, so can we just drop it?"

Diana struggles to rise out of her seat and moves forward as if heading towards the door. Dodi stands suddenly and blocks her way.

"This isn't about religion; this is about your attitude. I really don't know what to make of you at the moment Diana. One moment you're moping around all over the place, the next you're re- living the car crash and shooting, terrified that someone is out to get you and then you go and do something like this. I can't deny that I'm disappointed about your attitude towards going to the mosque, I really thought it might help sort you out, but then I'm disappointed in your attitude to pretty much everything at the moment."

Diana's eyes widen in shock at Dodi's words, before narrowing and flashing with temper
"Disappointed? Sort me out? I'm sorry if I'm not the perfect Muslim wife you were expecting Dodi. What would you like me to do? Start covering myself from head to toe and walking ten paces behind you?"

Diana spits out the words angrily and smiles at the look on Dodi's face when he hears them
"You know that's not what I want from you. What I want is a wife who knows how to behave, who has some respect for herself and the people that care about her."

Dodi holds his hands out as if imploring Diana to listen to him.
"And because I'm not going to the mosque I don't respect myself?"

Dodi sighs
"I didn't say that Diana, but you do have a point."

He looks at Diana's face and continues hurriedly
"It's just I saw how happy and excited you were after each time you went to the mosque. It seemed to be having

such a good effect on you and I'm disappointed that you're just letting that get away from you. And I can't understand how you seem to feel it's ok to leave the house for something as trivial as shopping, where you end up stressed and scared, but not to go the mosque, where you always come home relaxed and happy."

Dodi reaches out and places his hands on Diana's arms, which are folded tightly over the top of her bump. He lowers his voice and speaks softly

"I just want you happy. Is that too much to ask?"

He manoeuvres his head to try and meet Diana's eye, her gaze locked on the floor in front of her. He rubs his hands affectionately up and down her arms

"All I want is the best for you Diana. I want to keep you safe. Please help me to do that."

She raises her head slightly and offers him a small smile.

"I am sorry. Perhaps we could go out some time and look for some things for the baby together?"

Dodi looks at his watch then glances over at the mountain of things Diana returned from her shopping trip with, all strewn haphazardly across the room.

"It looks like you've got pretty much everything covered, except for furniture..."

Dodi's voice trails off as Diana looks embarrassed and avoids his eye

"...except I suppose that is coming at a later date."

He sighs loudly

"Well, I suppose we could talk about decorating the nursery together, unless you've already arranged that?"

Dodi has a twinkle in his eye that makes Diana laugh.
"And we'd better start moving your things over too."

Diana stares at Dodi with a confused look on her face
"My things?"

Dodi stares back, equally quizzically
"Yes. Your things. You didn't think we were going to have a baby and get married and continue to live in separate places did you?"

Diana thinks for a moment
"Well, I suppose not. I had thought that we wouldn't be living together until we got married, I didn't really stop to think about the baby coming and having the wedding plans on hold because of it."
"Speaking of which....."

Dodi lets the sentence hang in the air incomplete
"I know, I know. We really should set something down in stone, it's just that neither of us wanted it to seem like we were just getting married because I was pregnant, so I thought we'd just leave it on hold until after the baby arrives and think about it then."

Dodi's face looks sullen again
"You seem to have been doing a lot of thinking, yet this is the first I've heard about any of this."

Diana struggles to get out of the chair

"As much as I am enjoying this conversation, I need to make a trip to the bathroom. I trust it can wait until I get back?"

Her voice heavy with sarcasm, Diana does not wait for a response before leaving the room.

When she returns from the bathroom, Diana is smiling widely again, her hand pressed over her stomach. She laughs a little to herself as the baby moves inside of her and looks up to where Dodi had been sitting to share it with him. Her face falls as she finds the room empty. Slumping down into one of the sofas, Diana places her hands back over her stomach and waits to feel the baby moving again

"Come on little one. Cheer your mummy up. Let's have a little bit of movement, please?"

She looks down at her stomach as she speaks, rubbing her palm in soft circles over the now large bump. When nothing happens, Diana leans forward and begins to lightly massage her back, closing her eyes and dropping her head back as she eases her own discomfort. Moving her hands from her back, Diana relaxes back into the chair and begins to massage her temples.

The room is dark when Diana wakes up, clutching her hands to her stomach. She breathes in sharply, letting the air escape from her lungs slowly, before taking another deep breath.

"Oh not now. Please don't be now."

Diana struggles forward into a sitting position, breathing heavily as she does so. Her face contorts in pain and she pants slightly

"It can't be now. It's too early, I don't have anything ready."

Her face contorts again and she moans softly as her stomach contracts.

"Not now. Not now. Please not now. What do I do? Call the midwife. Call Dodi. Pack a bag. What do I need?"

Still in the darkness, Diana struggles to her feet and makes her way carefully across the room, swearing to herself as her shin makes contact with the edge of the coffee table. She stops at the doorframe, panting loudly as another contraction sweeps through her, causing her to double over in pain. She takes audible breaths, counting softly to herself until the pain passes before beginning to make her way out of the room again. Another contraction overtakes her on the stairs, causing her to sway slightly and grasp the banister in order to regain her balance. The house is still and quiet, the late hour meaning that all the staff are either sleeping or have gone home for the evening. Diana struggles to her bedroom, pushing the door open before collapsing on her bed and whimpering as the next contraction begins.

Once the pain has subsided, Diana rolls slowly off of the bed, testing her feet on the soft carpet before putting any weight on them. She makes her way to the wardrobe and pulls out a large weekend bag, dragging it to her chest of drawers and throwing in underwear and pyjamas. She stops suddenly in the middle of the room.

"The baby. I haven't got anything for the baby."

All the clothes she had purchased earlier still lie in the room Diana had woken up in, strewn across the floor. The essentials, such as nappies and wipes still remain unchecked on the 'to buy' list. Diana drops the half filled bag and makes her way to the phone. She picks up and dials a number hastily, waiting for someone to answer. When the call is finally connected, Diana shrieks at the groggy man on the phone, demanding that she speak to Dodi. When he answers the phone his voice is thick with sleep

"Diana? What is it?

Diana's words come out in a garbled rush

"Dodithebabyis onitsway."

It takes Dodi a few moments to process her words. Suddenly, his voice sounds clearer and more alert

"Are you sure?"

Diana snaps back at him.

"Yes I'm sure. And we haven't got any nappies or wipes or anything and it's taken me ages to get upstairs and now I've realised that all the clothes I bought are still downstairs."

Tears overtake Diana for the first time and she hiccoughs loudly. Dodi makes shushing noises down the phone

"Calm down darling, its fine. Wake up your staff, that is what they're there for. I'm on my way, I'll call the midwife and we'll get you to the hospital. Don't panic everything is going to be fine. I'll be there as fast as I can."

Diana makes a whimpering noise down the phone that Dodi seems to take as an agreement as he hangs up. Diana is left standing holding the receiver and listening to the dial tone as her waters break, sending liquid flooding down her legs.

CHAPTER TWENTY FOUR

Diana sucks loudly on the mouthpiece offered to her by the nurse and smiles as the gas and air take effect. Her eyes glaze over and the whimpering that she has been making during each contraction dies down to no more than a squeak. Dodi squeezes her hand

"How are you doing Diana? Are you ok?"

Diana smiles at him tightly, her face and forehead covered in a thin layer of sweat. She sucks hard at the mouthpiece again, whimpering slightly and closing her eyes

"Was that another one?"

Diana nods her head in response to Dodi's question. The nurse handing out the gas and air speaks to the couple

"We haven't been able to get hold of your midwife yet, but your contractions are getting fairly close together now. Is it ok if I examine you and we'll see how dilated you are and decide where to go from there?"

Dodi looks to Diana, who takes hold of his hand and grips tightly before nodding once. With laboured effort, Diana moves herself from the all fours position that she has placed herself into and lies on her back to allow the nurse to examine her. Pulling on a pair of gloves, the nurse carefully moves Diana's gown to one side before beginning her examination.

"You said that your waters had already gone?"

Diana nods her confirmation and the nurse smiles reassuringly at her

"Ok, well you're about five centimetres dilated, so we've still got a while to go yet."

She re-covers Diana and removes her gloves, tossing them into a clinical waste bin before addressing the couple again

"Sometimes, when it isn't the first baby, things can start to happen quite quickly. I'm going to try and reach your midwife again, but until then you just need to keep yourself as comfortable as you can get. We'll be in to check on you regularly, but if there is anything you need then just press the red button beside the bed."

The midwife smiles at the couple, who each manage a limp smile in response. Dodi stares at Diana, his brown eyes boring into her.

"Are you ok? Is there anything you need?"

Diana gestures for the gas and air and Dodi passes the mouthpiece to her, looking on in concern as she inhales from it deeply.

"Is the pain very bad? I know you said that you didn't want the epidural, but it's ok to change your mind. Do you want me to call the nurse back and ask her?"

Diana shakes her head and begins to manoeuvre herself back into the all fours position she had been occupying.

Dodi takes her arm to steady her, helping her rock back and forth.

"I picked up nappies and wipes on the way. I didn't know what ones we needed so I just got whichever ones I could see."

Dodi gestures to several carrier bags that are shoved underneath the plastic chairs in the corner of the room. Diana laughs softly when she sees how many bags have been placed there.

"You must have bought out the whole shop!"

Dodi blushes before replying with a hint of defiance

"Nothing is too much for my little boy."

Diana opens her mouth to respond, but instead places the mouthpiece inside and inhales deeply. She breathes slowly, still counting softly to herself until the pain subsides.

"Still so sure it's going to be a boy?"

Dodi laughs softly, as Diana continues

"You know, he, or she, still doesn't have a name."

Diana's face crumples in pain and she rocks back and forwards faster. Dodi leans towards her rubbing her back and murmuring softly until her face relaxes.

"The name will be there when the baby comes out, I'm sure of it."

Diana smiles weakly, before looking up as the door opens suddenly. The nurse re-enters the room, her face apologetic

"I'm afraid your midwife is with another couple in labour. She said she would leave them but they're having a difficult time. Do you have anyone else I can call for you?"

Diana and Dodi look at each other, before turning back to the nurse and each shaking their head.

"Well if it's ok with you, one of the staff here would be more than happy to step in."

Diana smiles gratefully at the nurse, before resuming her rocking and reaching once again for the gas and air. The nurse comes forward, brandishing a blood pressure monitor. Diana begins to move but the nurse places a hand on her arm to stop her.

"If that is where you're comfortable then I'll take it like that. Don't worry about moving yourself."

She smiles warmly at Diana before attaching the cuff to her arm and pumping away, before noting the reading down on a piece of paper.

"Your blood pressure is a bit high, has it been like that all through the pregnancy?"

Diana nods at the same time as Dodi replies

"Yes, it has been. We've been trying to let Diana relax as much as possible, but unfortunately she leads a very stressful life."

The glare that Diana aims at Dodi goes unnoticed by him, but not by the nurse. She continues awkwardly

"We're, erm, still waiting for your notes to be sent through, but am I right in thinking that the baby is early?"

Once again Dodi replies, with Diana shooting daggers at him

"Yes, several weeks. I think that may be stress related also."

"There are many reasons for an early labour. Whatever the cause, this baby is on the way, so let's just concentrate on getting it here safely, ok?"

Diana smiles gratefully at the nurse, who smiles back in response.

"Is there anything I can get for you? I'm afraid you can't really eat or drink, but a little bit of water is ok, if you'd like me to get you some?"

Diana nods once and struggles to speak as her face crumples in pain once again

"Yes. Water, please."

The nurse pats her reassuringly on the arm before leaving the room. Diana looks to Dodi, her face stricken

"Do you think the baby is going to be ok?"

Dodi leaves her side and begins to pace around the bed, Diana focusing on her rocking movements.

"The doctors and nurses don't seem worried, I don't think we have anything to worry about."

Diana looks up at Dodi, taking in his stance and the look on his face

"You think this is my fault."

Her voice is strained but the tone defiant. She stares at Dodi, forcing him to look at her.

"You think that I made the baby come early by getting myself into a state when I went out."

Dodi looks at her, his brown eyes focusing intently on her blue ones
"Diana, you're being ridiculous."

Diana takes a deep pull on her mouthpiece, rocking back and forwards, before responding.
"You do. I can tell from what you were saying to the nurse. All about me leading a stressful life. You think this is all my fault."

A tear slips down Diana's cheek as she gasps in pain and increases the tempo of her rocking. Dodi rushes to her side, rubbing her back as she moves.
"Don't be silly Diana, of course I don't think that. You need to stop working yourself up right now, just worry about what's happening."

Diana stops rocking and stares at him
"There you go again. Blaming me. Thinking that I'm messing things up for the baby that hasn't even arrived yet."

Dodi throws his hands up in the air in frustration.
"Can we not have this conversation now? Could we just leave our petty problems at the door and enjoy the birth of our child?"

Diana huffs in response and pulls again on the gas and air
"Glad you're enjoying it."

Dodi's response is lost as Diana lets out her loudest wail yet, causing the nurse to rush into the room. She places her hand on Diana's back, before talking to her in a soothing motion

"Was that a painful one love? Can I just get you back on to your back and have another look at you, see how you're doing?"

The nurse and Dodi each take Diana by the elbow and help her up into a sitting position. Diana stays like that for several moments, breathing deeply, before relaxing on to her back and parting her legs. The nurse once again pulls on her gloves, before rubbing a small amount of gel across her fingertips and beginning to examine Diana. She smiles widely before pulling her gloves off and tossing them in the bin.

"I think we're almost there. Diana if you want to change your mind about the epidural then now is the time to do it."

Dodi stares at Diana as she shakes her head in response.
"No. I can do it."

Her voice is strained and her face exhausted, but Diana smiles weakly at Dodi and the nurse. Dodi looks concerned

"Are you sure? There is no shame in changing your mind. No one is going to judge you."

Diana's face creases up in pain once more but she shakes her head defiantly. The nurse smiles.

"Ok, well I'm going to stay with you now until this baby makes an appearance."

She pats Diana's hand reassuringly
"Anything you need, I'll be here for."

Dodi smiles gratefully at the nurse as Diana breaks into another ear splitting wail.

Diana smiles adoringly down at the tiny bundle wrapped tightly in her arms. Her blonde hair is matted and even darker circles than normal are etched around her eyes. Dodi sits in the corner of the room, staring at the pair.

"You're stunning."

Diana looks up at him and smiles
"He looks just like you. His skin is a bit lighter, it's the colour of coffee. And look at all his hair!"

Dodi grins at Diana
"And his eyelashes, they're so long! His eyes are brown, of course, the little we've seen of them so far."

Dodi steps out of his chair and walks towards Diana and the baby
"Is it alright if I hold him now?"

Diana looks up at Dodi and blushes softly
"Sorry, I just got caught up in looking at him. He's so beautiful."

She moves her arms slowly, handing over the bundle of white blankets and baby to Dodi, who holds the boy as if he is made of china. He stares for a few moments, before looking back at Diana, who is focused intently on the pair

"I can see you in him too you know. He's got your nose. And your chin."

Diana smiles widely and stretches up to catch another look at her newborn son
"Do you think so?"

Dodi, who has resumed staring at the baby, smiles and nods without looking up. He begins to walk gingerly around the room, stepping softly and rocking his arms back and forth with the gentlest motions. Diana watches, fascinated, and neither of them speak for several minutes.
"He needs a name."

Diana's words are soft, the smile not moving from her face.
"I was just thinking that."

Dodi smiles at Diana. When he speaks his voice is hesitant, as if afraid Diana might take badly to his suggestion
"What about Kamil? I've had it in my mind for a while. It means perfect in Arabic."

Diana's smile stretches further across her face.
"He *is* perfect."

There is laughter in her tone. Dodi smiles warmly at her before looking down at his son
"Kamil? Is that your name?"

The baby makes a small snuffling noise in his sleep causing both Diana and Dodi to laugh

"Kamil it is."

Diana stares at Dodi and they both smile widely
   "Can his middle name be Edward? After my father?"

Dodi does not look up as he replies
   "Of course it can. Kamil Edward Al Fayed. It has a nice ring to it, doesn't it?"

Diana shuffles forward to the edge of the bed, next to where Dodi is cradling the baby, and peeps into the bundle in his arms. All wrapped in white, Kamil lies sleeping, long dark eyelashes lying flat against his caramel coloured skin. A mop of hair, only a shade darker than his skin, pokes erratically out of the top of the blankets. Dodi leans forward and kisses the boy softly on the top of the head before handing him over to Diana and kissing her forehead. He smiles widely at the pair.
   "I'm just nipping out, there are lots of phone calls that need to be made."

Diana beams as Dodi makes his way out of the room, before staring back down at her newborn son, rocking him back and forth and humming to him softly.

CHAPTER TWENTY FIVE

Diana looked down at baby Kamil and gasped. She stares incredulous at Dodi

"What happened to his hair?"

Let out of the hospital the previous day, Dodi had left Diana to rest at his house, telling Diana he was taking the baby to visit his family. He had been gone for the best part of the day and when he returned the baby's once luscious dark hair was gone. Dodi mutters in response.

"Sunnah. Muslim tradition."

Diana stares at Dodi, who avoids her gaze.

"I'm sorry, what? You'll have to explain that a little bit more."

Diana sounds as if she is struggling to keep her voice calm. Dodi sighs theatrically and moves his head to meet her gaze.

"It is an Islamic tradition. Sunnah. Seven days after a baby is born, his head is shaved and weighed and then the same amount in gold is donated to charity."

Diana considers his words for a moment, looking slightly appeased, before anger clouds her features again.

"And you didn't think to tell me this before you left. Perhaps I wanted to be there? Or at least be consulted on the matter?"

She strokes the sleeping boys head and adds wistfully, almost to herself

"All his beautiful hair."

Dodi looks abashed and holds his hands out apologetically

"I didn't want to bring up the whole religion thing again, we've been getting on so well recently. It's for charity, and it will grow back."

Diana stares down at the baby and sighs heavily.

"I suppose so. Still, it would have been nice to be asked."

Dodi walks over to Diana and their son and wraps his arms around the pair, kissing Diana on the side of her head.

"I'm sorry. I didn't think."

Diana smiles in response and the pair both stare down at the sleeping bundle in Diana's arms. Pursing his puffy pink lips, Kamil's eyes shoot open and their dark muddy brown stare at his mother and father before he breaks into an ear splitting wail.

"I gave him some milk less than an hour ago, so he can't be hungry already."

Dodi looks perplexed, and breaks away to allow Diana to place the baby over her shoulder in a loving gesture. The pair both wrinkle their noses at the same time.

"Time for a clean nappy I think."

Diana says the words with a smile on her face and begins to move towards the door. Dodi moves into her way and reaches out for Kamil.

"Don't worry, I'll do it."

Diana smiles in response, but clutches the baby close to her.

"It's ok. You've had him all afternoon. It'll be nice to have some time just the two of us, won't it Kamil?"

Diana looks at the baby, who is still whimpering softly and smiles before kissing him softly on the top of the head.

"I really don't mind."

Dodi's tone is insistent and Diana shoots him a strange look before making her way around him and out of the room.

Dodi winces at Diana's shriek, heard clearly from downstairs in the living room. She flies down the stairs, Kamil over her shoulder, still naked.

"What have you done to him?"

She brandishes the baby in midair, exposing his full nakedness to Dodi. He holds out his hands to take the boy but Diana snatches him away, cradling him protectively to her chest.

"Now I know why you didn't talk to me about today, you didn't want to tell me that you were planning on mutilating our child."

Diana hurls the words out like weapons, stepping away from Dodi as she does so.

"Diana, relax. It's not that big a deal. Having a boy circumcised is always done at the same time the head is shaved. It just makes more sense to get it all done in one go."

"But you hadn't even discussed it with me! Hadn't even asked for my opinion. Don't you think I might have had something to say about the fact that you were planning on having surgery done on my child?"

When Dodi doesn't respond Diana's face takes on a knowing look

"That's it, isn't it? You didn't want to give me the chance to say no."

Dodi looks at her imploringly

"I didn't want to start a fight, like I said. I told you that the baby was going to be indoctrinated into Islam. That means performing all the rites that go along with it. All the things that are always done when we welcome a new child into the community."

"I said you could take the baby to the mosque, I never agreed to any of this."

Diana gestures dramatically towards the baby with her free arm, holding Kamil close to her with the other arm. When Dodi responds he speaks to her slowly, as if she is a child

"It's all part and parcel Diana. If you had bothered to pay attention you would know this."

"Don't give me that. We never discussed circumcision, or shaving the baby's head. You just went ahead and did whatever you wanted because you think that you know best. That you're so pious, while I'm just ignorant. I can't believe you thought you could just go off with Kamil and do whatever you wanted."

Kamil opens his eyes and stares at his mother for half a second before bursting into tears. Diana glares at Dodi

"Now look what you've done."

Dodi looks incredulous

"Me? You're the one shouting and screaming. All I was trying to do was the best by my son, I don't know why you have such a problem with that."

"Our son. And I have a problem with you going behind my back and doing whatever the hell you like in the name of religion. I have a problem with you making decisions that will affect our son forever without you even discussing them with me."

Diana shifts Kamil in her arms, rocking him softly in an attempt to try and soothe his tears. Dodi opens his mouth to respond but Diana holds up her hand and cuts him off

"I don't even want to hear it right now Dodi, I'm so angry."

Her eyes penetrate him, glaring ice cold. Dodi does not try to speak again, but avoids Diana's gaze. She stares at him for a few more minutes, before noticing a wet patch against her chest. She holds Kamil out and groans theatrically to the baby

"Christ. My fault for not putting a nappy on you I suppose."

Dodi looks up at her and smiles, hoping to join in with the amusement, but Diana stares at him coldly. She kisses the top of Kamil's bald head and holds him close to her sodden top before making her way out of the room without looking at Dodi.

Upstairs Diana gently bathes Kamil's skin, wiping him dry before fixing a clean nappy on to him. She hums softly, trying to keep the tone of her voice even as a lone tear slips down her cheek. Kamil fixes his big brown eyes on her sleepily, blinking several times before finally slipping off to sleep.

Carefully taking hold of him, Diana places him gently in his crib and watches over him for several seconds to make sure his rest is undisturbed. The tears are now flowing down her cheeks, but this time Diana makes no move to try and halt them, letting them drip freely onto the blankets covering Kamil. In his sleep the baby whimpers softly and Diana leans forward and strokes his cheek until he calms, careful that no errant tears disturb his dreams. Once she seems sure that he is settled, Diana makes her way over to the corner of the room and removes her stained blouse. Throwing it into Kamil's laundry pile, she wipes down her skin and hunts around for something to cover herself with. Picking up a discarded blanket, Diana wraps it around herself and settles down on the feeding chair next to Kamil's crib. Still crying silent tears, Diana watches her son sleep, occasionally reaching out as if to touch his head, before drawing her hand back to her chest. She flinches as she hears the front door slam; looking down at the baby as if to make sure that the noise has not interrupted his sleep. Kamil lets out several tiny snuffling noises but his eyes remain tightly closed. Tucking her legs underneath herself, Diana seems to fight off sleep, forcing her eyes open several times as the lids droop heavily. The well of tears now dry, Diana sits lifelessly in the chair staring down at the sleeping baby as if in some sort of trace. Her face is chalky white, the dark rings circling her eyes seemingly having taken up permanent residence there. Shivering slightly despite the warmth of the room, Diana wraps the blanket tighter around her, covering up her bare skin and keeps vigil, waiting for Kamil to awake.

William holds the tiny baby close to him and stares down at the bundle. Harry peers over his brother's shoulder and looks down at the newest addition to the family.

"Was I that small when I was born?"

Diana smiles warmly, although neither boy notices that the smile does not quite reach to her eyes

"You were a little bit bigger, you arrived only a few days early, where as Kamil surprised us all."

Both William and Harry smile in response and look again at their new baby brother.

"Are you disappointed that it's another boy?"

Harry's question hangs in the air, he and William staring at their mother while she tries to find the right words to respond.

"No, of course not. I have always wanted a girl, but how could I be disappointed with a boy when the others have turned out so perfectly?"

Harry beams at his mother

"Dodi said that Kamil means perfect."

Diana looks at William, who is staring intently at Kamil

"When did he tell you that?"

William still does not look at Diana. Instead he untucks Kamil's tightly wrapped blankets and tries to worm his index finger into the baby's clenched fist.

"When he called us to tell us that you'd had the baby. He said you were calling him Kamil and that it meant perfect."

Diana stares at William open mouthed for a moment. Still intent on Kamil, William does not notice.

"I thought he called you almost straight after, while Kamil was being weighed?"

William stares up at Diana, momentarily giving up his quest

"That's right, because someone told me I had to ask about how much the baby weighed, but I asked Dodi and he said he didn't know yet. Why?"

Diana struggles to hide her fury and smiles at William's quizzical face

"No reason. And yes, Kamil does mean perfect."

William motions to Harry to sit down on the sofa and gently hands over their baby brother. Harry sits poker straight with the baby in his arms, as if afraid of breaking him. William smiles at his brothers face before making his way over to sit next to their mother.

"Is everything alright?"

Diana wraps her arms around her eldest son and draws him close to her.

"Of course it is. I'm surrounded by all of my boys, how could it not be?"

Diana smiles another smile that does not quite reach her eyes

"It's just that you were quite vague about where Dodi is, I thought that something might be wrong?"

Diana blushes slightly and tries to cover it with a wide smile

"Having a baby is a very stressful experience, I'm probably just a bit tired and a bit vague in general. Nothing to worry about I promise."

William does not look convinced and opens his mouth as if to protest when Kamil lets out a loud wail. Harry's face immediately takes on a stricken look

"I didn't do anything!"

William and Diana both laugh softly, and Diana checks her watch

"It's alright, it's just been a while since he last ate. He's probably just hungry."

Harry's face sags in relief and he gratefully hands Kamil over to Diana, who leans down to kiss Harry's head. She looks from Harry to William and back again

"You know I love you all more than anything in this world."

Harry looks embarrassed, but William's face takes on a look of concern. Before he can speak, Diana smiles widely and whisks Kamil out of the room to feed him.

CHAPTER TWENTY SIX

Diana looks over at Kamil sleeping in his crib, before picking up the phone. She presses the handset to her ear firmly and listens to the dial tone for several seconds. Over in his crib, Kamil stirs and Diana places the phone back on the hook and rushes to his side. Eyes closed firmly and still sleeping soundly, Diana watches over her son for a few moments. When he does not stir again she tucks his blankets around him and heads back to the phone. Sitting herself down on the chair next to the phone table, Diana stares at the implement as if waiting for it to ring of its own accord. When nothing happens she once again picks up the receiver, reaching out to dial. One number, two. Diana hangs up the phone and resumes her staring match, playing absentmindedly with the coil connecting the receiver to the base. Taking a deep breath she picks up the phone again, managing three numbers before giving in and slamming the phone down. Getting out of her seat, Diana begins pacing the room, fiddling with her hair and attempting to focus intently on her sleeping child. Every few steps her eyes involuntarily wander back to the phone, her path of pacing edging ever closer. Finally, summoning a deep breath, Diana sits herself down, picks up the handset and dials hurriedly, her hand shaking as she does so. She presses the receiver tightly to her ear as if to try and suppress the shaking and listens as the line on the other end rings repeatedly. After ten rings, Diana hangs up the phone, her face dejected, and slowly makes her way over to the crib where Kamil is still sleeping.

"Looks like no one is home, doesn't it poppet?"

She reaches out and strokes the baby's soft cheek gently, running her finger underneath his now well filled out chin. Kamil sighs in his sleep and Diana smiles sadly.

"Just me and you again, hey sweetheart? That's how we like it anyway."

Her voice waivers as she speaks, as if she is trying to convince herself more than the unknowing, sleeping child in front of her. Diana breathes deeply, her blue eyes filling up with tears. Before they can spill over, the phone rings loudly, the noise shattering the near silence of the whole house. Diana rushes to the handset, her eyes fixed firmly on Kamil.

"Hello?"

Diana's voice is barely more than a whisper, her gaze still focused on the sleeping child.

"Did you call?"

The voice on the phone is refined, a deep male baritone with a cut glass accent. Diana sits hurriedly in the chair next to the phone and opens her mouth, clearly struggling to form a response.

"I, erm, well, yes. I did."

When the man on the phone does not speak again, Diana continues.

"I was hoping we could meet."

Her voice is soft, the words tumbling out hurriedly

"I know things haven't been the best between us, for quite a while actually, but I need someone to talk to and you were the only person I could think of."

Diana glances once again to baby Kamil, who is beginning to stir in his crib.

"Now isn't the best time for me to talk actually. Please, can we meet?"

The man on the other end of the phone sighs deeply.

"I'm not sure that that is the best idea."

Diana looks back at Kamil, whose brown eyes are now wide open and searching the room.

"Please?"

Her voice is imploring and seems to have some effect on the man, who pauses before relenting

"I suppose so. The usual place?"

Diana's face lights up at his agreement and readily agrees.

"Yes, that would be perfect. Tomorrow?"

The frostiness at the start of the conversation seems to have dissolved as the man on the end of the phone laughs.

"I have an engagement in the morning, but I am free in the afternoon if you insist on meeting so soon. I'm still not sure that it is the wisest plan, but I can be there by three."

Diana's smile is cut short by a wail from Kamil, now fully awake in his crib.

"I'd better go. I'll see you at three."

She does not wait for a response, but hangs up the phone and rushes to the crib. Kamil stops crying as soon as Diana scoops him up and holds him close to her, rocking softly. Her smile returns as soon as the baby stops crying and Diana begins to pace around the room, bouncing softly and enjoying the smiles from her baby boy.

"Is it time for feeding already Kamil? You're such a hungry boy! You've certainly got your daddies appetite."

Diana's face clouds over at her own mention of Dodi and she presses Kamil closer to her to hide her face from him.

"Let's get you changed and then we'll see about getting you something to eat."

Diana places Kamil gently on to the changing table and begins to change the baby's nappy, smiling as Kamil kicks his legs and coos softly.

Diana sits down on the bench, and sighs softly before speaking
    "Thank you for agreeing to see me."

The man next to her shifts uncomfortably, his light jacket and trousers perfectly matched and auburn hair ruffling softly in the breeze.
    "What do you want Diana?"

She stares at him in amazement,
    "I said I needed someone to talk to, is that so hard to believe?"

He focuses his dark eyes intently on Diana, before looking away and staring intently at his shoes

"You said some pretty hurtful things."

"With good reason!"

Diana focuses intently on the man, who still avoids her gaze

"I apologised for what I did. I was angry, hurt, that you had just cut me out of your life like that. I lashed out, and regretted it later."

Diana speaks softly

"You know why I had to do that, we'd spoken about it."

"Just because we'd talked about it doesn't mean I was prepared to just end it all overnight. I was shocked. I was hurt. You broke my heart."

Diana stares at the man seated next to her, who avoids her gaze. She reaches out to take his large, calloused hand in her petite delicate one and the two sit in silence for several minutes. In the distance horses gallop across the large field, held in by expansive wooden fencing. The couple focus on the animals, not looking at each other but their hands still entwined. A cold wind sweeps across the landscape and Diana shivers

"Here, take my coat."

He is on his feet and removing his jacket in an instant, but Diana protests vehemently

"You'll be freezing. I'm alright, it's just this sitting about. It's no good for old bones like mine."

She laughs self consciously as the man seated next to her takes a long appraisal of her

"You look pretty good for old bones."

Diana blushes scarlet and looks away, but does not let go of his hand. When she does not reply he continues

"You said that you needed someone to talk to?"

Diana looks up again at the man and seems to realise for the first time that her hand is clasping his. She releases her hold as if stung and clutches her hands together in her lap, staring at them intently. He reaches out, across to her lap and gently prises her hands apart, taking one back softly into his own embrace.

"It's ok Diana, you can talk to me."

His reassuring words are backed up by the sincere look in his deep brown eyes, staring solemnly into Diana's morose blue ones. Diana mumbles something to herself.

"Pardon? I didn't quite catch that."

Diana sighs loudly and repeats herself

"I said, I shouldn't be here."

Shifting slightly in his seat, the man chuckles to himself in a deep tenor

"Well, I did tell you on the phone that I didn't think that meeting up would be a good idea, but I have to say, now that we're here, I'm rather thrilled."

Diana flicks her head up sharply and studies the face staring intently at her, as if searching for sincerity in his handsome face. Clearly pleased with what she finds, Diana looks away and replies in a small voice

"Me too."

Sighing and leaning back against the bench, pushing out his chest in the manner of a man who has just finished a large meal, he surveys the countryside for a moment before speaking again

"I take it things with Dodi aren't going so well."

Diana is frozen for a moment, her mouth half open as if she had been getting ready to deny the accusation before she thought better of it. He offers, in way of explanation,

"You wouldn't be here if they were."

Diana slumps back in her seat, focusing intently on one of the horses in the distance and does not respond. He tries again

"I just want to be here for you. I hate seeing you like this."

Diana's eyes fill up with tears and she buries her face into the man's chest as he wraps his arms comfortingly around her. Softly he strokes her hair and whispers words of encouragement to her.

It is several minutes before Diana has collected her thoughts enough to extract herself from his embrace and when she does she looks embarrassed

"Oh god, I'm so sorry. I don't know what came over me."

Diana bends down and rummages in her handbag for a tissue and begins dabbing at her eyes and nose, seemingly in an effort to avoid the man's penetrative gaze.

"Talk to me."

His words are soft but forceful, and Diana stares up at him, all the willpower seeming to dissolve right out of her blue eyes. She begins slowly, but once she starts the words seem to take on a life of their own, tumbling out of her mouth

"It's all been so horrible. He makes decisions as if I don't exist, like my opinion doesn't even matter. I said he could take Kamil to the mosque and he agreed that I could take him to church if I wanted to, but he's done all of these Islamic ceremonies with him and they go down to the mosque a couple of times a week. I know it's probably my fault for not taking Kamil to church, but I mentioned about having him christened the other day and Dodi was furious. He said I couldn't indoctrinate the boy into two religions and that he had taken care of Kamil's spiritual wellbeing and that it wasn't something I needed to concern myself with."

Diana's eyes fill up and overflow with tears as she is speaking. The man sits next to her in silence, reaching out for her hand as the tears begin streaming. Diana looks up at him, making no attempt to stem the rivers of moisture running down her cheeks

"Did you know that he had him circumcised? Without telling me! He just came home after taking Kamil out and the poor baby came back with all his hair shaved off. When I asked about it Dodi just told me that it was a Muslim tradition, then the next time I changed Kamil's nappy I noticed that he'd had that done too! What sort of parent does things like that to a child without speaking to the other parent about it?"

Diana's voice waivers as she speaks through heavily flowing tears

"That's what they do though, isn't it? Muslim men are the decision makers of the family, they have certain traditions to follow."

"So you're saying that this is what I deserve for getting involved with a Muslim man?"

Diana's words are defiant but the emotion does not reflect in her face, which looks weighed upon.

"I didn't mean it like that, like it's a negative thing. I'm just saying that maybe you should look at it from Dodi's point of view. How old is Kamil now, six months?"

Diana nods her head once in confirmation

"So he's probably just doing all the things with a new baby that every Muslim dad does. He probably doesn't even think about it, it's just natural."

"He'd picked out Kamil's name and told people before even talking to me about it, then sweet talked me into agreeing."

Diana looks up to gauge the reaction of her words, as if she had been holding this piece of information back. The man sighs and puts his arm around her

"I can understand that you're hurt about all these things Diana. Have you tried talking to Dodi about them?"

Diana sighs in defeat

"He just says that if I was interested then I'd go to the mosque with both of them, which I'm more than welcome to do apparently."

"What happened to your visits to the mosque? I only know what I read in the paper, and we all know how accurate they are."

Diana stares at him coldly
"As you would know."

He regards her with equal despair
"There have been plenty of inaccuracies reported about me. I'll have you know that some rather nasty stuff has been said about me, all of which since reports of our relationship emerged."

Diana looks abashed for a moment, before adding
"It wasn't all lies. There were a few home truths in there."

The pair regard each other in silence for a few moments, letting Diana's accusation hang in the air.
"Well, I think we've said all we've got to say here."

The man raises himself up off of the bench, Diana grasping on to his sleeve as he begins to walk away.
"Don't go. I'm sorry, I shouldn't have said that."

He stops moving but makes no effort to sit back down
"The boys miss you, Harry especially."

Diana's words are soft, faltering slightly as she speaks. He sits down suddenly, this time it is he who is avoiding her gaze
"Christ Diana, that's hardly fair."

They sit in silence again, the cold wind sweeping across the open spaces. Diana shivers and looks at her watch

"Oh god, look at the time. I said I'd be back half an hour ago."

A distinct look of relief washes across the man's face and he rises back into a standing position and offers Diana his arm to help her up.

"It was, as ever, a pleasure."

He smiles, although his eyes remain clouded as if he has many things on his mind. Diana throws her arms around him, catching him by surprise.

"Thank you for seeing me. I hope we can do it again soon."

Not waiting for an answer, Diana releases him from her embrace and begins walking towards her car, leaving him staring at her rapidly diminishing figure, his face a mixture of confusion and sadness.

CHAPTER TWENTY SEVEN

I'm so excited! It's been six months since Arun kissed me and things have just been amazing. We've been seeing each other as often as possible, around both our uni work of course. And not at the Mosque. We thought we'd keep things quiet there for a while, keep our relationship to ourselves until we knew how serious it was going to be. I mean, of course I knew how serious it was going to be, but you can never tell a man that, can you? Sure fire way to scare them off. Anyway, he's still been teaching me about Islam, just not quite as often as we've been telling people he has. What with all the protests going on around the country about Diana and Dodi's relationship earlier in the year as well. Almost everyone at the mosque has been friendly to me since I started going there, but you never know what some people really think do you? I bet Diana didn't realise that there would be protests around the country just because she fell in love.

Anyway, it's been six months so we've decided to tell everyone that we're a couple. We talked about it and it's pretty obvious to everyone that I'm serious about Islam now, there is no way that they could think that I'm only interested because it's fashionable. Though it is still in the news a lot. Even though Diana hasn't been seen at a Mosque for a while, once the baby's name was released everyone started saying that since the baby was clearly going to be raised a Muslim and then it wouldn't be long before Diana followed suit. Kamil is pretty adorable. I think that any people who were unsure about Diana and what she was doing with Dodi soon changed their mind when they saw his perfect little face. And Diana and Dodi looked so happy when they came out of the hospital, smiling like two really proud parents. Kamil is a nice name too, I think I read somewhere that it means perfect or something like that. It got me thinking about what my kids would look like if Arun and I had a baby together. He or she would probably have similar sort of colouring to Kamil, the dark eyes and the caramel coloured skin. I asked him what he thought about it and you should have seen the look on his face. I should have known better than to mention even hypothetical babies to a man. It did lead to the 'where is this relationship going' conversation though, which was when we decided that we'd start telling people about us after six months, so it's not all bad. It got me thinking about baby names as well. There is this woman who has been in the paper recently, a wife of one of the cabinet members, I forget which one. Anyway, she converted to Islam pretty much as soon as the first picture of Diana at a Mosque came out. Jumped right on the bandwagon. It caused a pretty big stir actually, someone so high ranking suddenly converting to Islam. She cashed right in on it as well, giving interviews with a couple of glossy magazines and talking about her new found spiritualism. Her husband even ended up having to defend her in the House of Commons, when people started complaining that she was behaving in a manor unbefitting a wife of a Cabinet Minister. If you ask me that sort of attitude is no better than those Muslims who took to the streets to protest about Diana. Religion is a personal quest and people should be able to find their own path without being influenced by anyone else. Not that some people aren't just doing it because of Diana. Even I know that I wouldn't be where I am today if it wasn't for her influence, but at least I'm doing it for the right reasons. When I went home a few weeks ago there was even an article in my mother's Women's Own magazine about Islam, with an accompanying pull out about the most flattering way to keep yourself covered up and retain your modesty. It's verging on the ridiculous. Anyway, this Ministers wife has been in the papers more than usual because she has just given birth to a baby girl. A baby girl she has decided to call Aakifah. By all accounts it means devoted or dedicated or something like that, a fact she was keen to get across when she did that huge interview and photo shoot for Hello! Magazine. (I bought it purely for research purposes, obviously) She's totally just jumping on the Diana bandwagon, first with her conversion and then secondly with picking a 'profound' Muslim name for her child. The only flaw in her plan is the boring white Christian husband really. Poor little baby girl is the whitest little blue eyed blonde you've ever seen and she's got to live with that name for the rest of her life. If it was me, not that I've been thinking about it at all really, I'd go for something a bit more classic. Jamal is quite nice, something that could easily be shortened too. Or Aisha for a girl. It's really pretty and it's the name of one of the Prophet Muhammad's wives, so it's got important religious connotations, which I think is important.

Arun arrived about half an hour earlier than he needed to and we just sat on the sofa talking and kissing. He knew how nervous I was about what people at the mosque would think about me and just kept reassuring me that it was going to be ok. At first it was him who didn't want to tell people, I think he was worried about what his parents would think about him being with a white girl. There are no secrets at the mosque. Eventually I won him around though, I pointed out that if we were going to keep seeing each other then wouldn't it be better for us to tell everyone rather than just having them find out? He couldn't argue with that. And it has been quite a while that I've been going to the mosque now. Definitely long enough so that people don't think I'm only going to show interest while Islam is trendy. So now we're going to tell people that we're a couple. Today. I thought long and hard about what would be the best thing to wear, what make up to put on and how I should do my hair. I even went back and had a look at some of the clippings I made of Diana and her visits to the mosque, just to get an idea. In the end I settled on some smart trousers and a long sleeved jumper. It can be pretty cold inside some of the rooms in the mosque, what with all the pale wood and big open spaces. I said this out to Arun but he only laughed and told me that was the way all mosques are. I suppose I've still got quite a lot to learn in some ways. It's pretty frustrating that I still have to have my lessons. Arun has kept up my teaching, he said it would look strange if he suddenly decided to give up. At first it was a really good excuse for us to just get some time alone together, but then he decided that he'd better keep on actually teaching me things, if I was serious about Islam. Which obviously I am. It's just still really difficult to concentrate when he's sitting so close to me with those big brown eyes and oh so soft lips.

"Hadn't we better get going?"

I look at the time and realise that he's right. It's so easy to get distracted when he's around, even if I am still incredibly nervous. He gets up off of the sofa and pulls me by the hand

"Come on, we don't want to be late now, do we?"

I get up reluctantly and he pulls me into a warm embrace, his chin resting lightly on the top of my head. I sigh and bury my face into his chest

"Are you sure we're doing the right thing?"

I don't look at him as I speak, but he breaks away from me and takes my chin to force my gaze to meet his

"Hey, come on. This was your idea, remember?"

"I know, but what if they don't approve? Don't think I'm good enough for you?"

He hugs me again

"It's not about what they think though, is it? It's about what I think. And no one will think that anyway. You've proved that you're just as dedicated as anyone there. Just as committed."

I blush a bit and try not to think about the times I've gone shopping instead of doing the studying that I promised him I'd do, or the lessons wasted daydreaming about him. Still, it doesn't mean I'm not dedicated, just easily distracted. And I'm working on it.

We didn't talk much on the walk to the mosque. Just held hands. I couldn't help but constantly look around for people we knew. It feels weird to be out and about together in the day time after so long of hiding our relationship. We didn't see anyone before we got to the mosque, but we were spotted straight away as soon as we got there. Arun tightened his grip on my hand and gave it a little squeeze to reassure me. I thought it was going to be ok as well because the first person we saw was Jameela. I raised my free hand and gave her a wave but she just glared at me and then stormed off. I did wonder how she felt about Arun, she'd seemed a little put out that it was him who was giving me private lessons, but she never said anything about liking him so I'd assumed that he was fair game. I'd never intentionally go after a guy that I know one of my friends liked. Not that Jameela and I are that close anyway. But if she'd said something then I definitely would have stayed away. Probably. I guess I didn't give her much chance though, what with keeping our relationship a secret and all. I'll have to talk to her at some point.

"What was up with Jameela?"

God, men can be so dense sometimes.
"Nothing, don't worry about it."

I smile at Arun. By this point we've made it into the ground of the mosque and a few more people are starting to pay attention. No one says anything, not even friendly greetings which even I usually get by this point. I'd kind of expected that though, I suppose us being together is a bit of a shock. We walk past a few of the women who were so cold to me when I first started coming here and I smile hopefully, because they've been almost nice to me recently. They ignore me and start whispering as soon as our backs have turned. Still, who cares what they think? I tighten my hold on Arun's hand, his grip was starting to slip but I guess that's just because I'm walking a bit slower than he is. He does seem in an awful hurry to get inside today. Probably because it's so cold. I up my pace to keep up with him, tucking my free arm across me and underneath his. Normally he'd look down and smile at me, but he keeps his eyes fixed firmly ahead, on the entrance we are aiming for. I guess he was more nervous than he let on earlier. Still, it was nice of him to try and be brave for my sake. A couple of groups are actually openly pointing now, and making no effort to keep their voices down. Some people are so rude! I can't actually hear what they're saying because of the wind but I guess that it's not very nice. You'd think that there would be a little more open mindedness in today's day and age, what with Diana paving the way and all. Still, I'm sure in time everyone will be fine with it. It's probably just a little bit of a shock. We've made it through the main doors now and I look up at Arun and smile, but he's still staring straight ahead. I move the arm across me and bend down to take off my shoes, still holding his hand. As I straighten up I can see the Imam standing in front of us, his face cold and disapproving. I straighten my shoulders, ready to defend our relationship, but Arun drops my hand as if he's been burnt, a guilty look on his face.

CHAPTER TWENTY EIGHT

"Have you seen this?"

Diana glares at Dodi over the top of the newspaper. Concentrating intently on the cup of coffee in his hand he does not respond, instead raising a piece of toast to his mouth and taking a large bite. Diana shakes the newspaper in frustration.

"I said, have you seen this?"

Dodi looks up at her, his face cold, and maintains eye contact as he lifts his cup and takes a long drink.

"Very mature. So you're just going to ignore me indefinitely?"

Dodi sighs and puts down his coffee cup,

"I don't see any point in having the same conversations, the same arguments, over and over again."

"I wasn't trying to start an argument. I wasn't even going to mention anything like that. I was just asking you if you had seen what is in the newspaper."

Diana's voice sounds as if she is struggling to keep it even, her eyes glancing repeatedly to Kamil, who is perched in his high chair at the end of the table. Oblivious to his parent's discussion, he is happily attempting to feed himself a combination of yoghurt and banana, most of which seems to be embedded in his thick dark hair.

"I have, but I don't want to talk about it. I don't want to have that conversation again."

Dodi also seems to be struggling with his tone, the words coming out strangled and low. Diana opens her mouth to respond, but Dodi gestures to Kamil

"Would you look at the state of him. Please Diana, he's too little to feed himself."

Diana gets up from her chair defiantly and attempts to mop up some of the yoghurt from Kamil's forehead.

"How else is he supposed to learn Dodi? He's a baby, they're supposed to make a mess!"

Kamil beams at his mother and bashes his plastic spoon on the bowl in front of him happily. Diana returns the grin, mopping at more yoghurt before returning to her seat and picking up her coffee cup. She gestures to the paper again

"So we're just not going to talk about this?"

Wordlessly, a member of staff enters the room and begins to clear away the breakfast things from the table, careful to avoid eye contact with either Dodi or Diana. Both of them stare at her in silence until she leaves the room, before continuing their conversation

"No, we're not. Because it's the same discussion again and again and frankly I'm sick of it."

Dodi keeps his voice low as if afraid of being overheard, and rises from the table as he speaks.

"I'm going to work. We're having dinner with my family this evening. Make sure you and Kamil are ready by the time I get home."

Diana pulls a face at Kamil, who lets out a deep chuckle. Dodi glares at Diana, before picking up his briefcase and suit jacket and making his way out of the room. Staying seated at the table, Diana absentmindedly hands Kamil his juice cup, once again poring over the newspaper.

"Christ, where do they get all of this stuff from?"

Diana mutters to herself, as Kamil has gone back to banging loudly on his bowl, gurgling along happily to his own music.

The newspaper is filled with stories on Diana, prompted by an opportune photographer managing to snap a picture actually inside of the Mosque with Kamil. Smiling and chatting happily to some of the women there, Diana looks calm and relaxed in the picture. The headline printed alongside the picture and subsequent story speculates that Diana is on the verge of officially announcing her conversion to Islam. Almost half of the entire newspaper is taken up with the story and spin off articles from important members of the Islamic community and people who claim to be in Diana's inner circle. In the centre of the newspaper there is a two page interview given by Samantha Campbell, wife of Martin Campbell, MP for Southall. A recent Islamic convert, she tells of the events in her life that lead her to Islam, the birth of her daughter and her attempts to convert her husband. In the middle of the page, in bold print, the newspaper has made a feature out of a quote given by the woman

"I credit Diana for showing me the way to Islam and I'm sure many other people will feel the same."

Diana had read through the interview twice, her face sinking further and further into disbelief, before bringing it up with Dodi. Now she once again goes through the interview, muttering to herself

"I've barely even met the woman. I've certainly never spoken to her."

On the following page the newspaper lists the growth in popularity for Islam, citing the trend across the globe. Diana sighs and leans her head on the table.

"Maybe I'll let them get a picture of me picking my nose and we'll see if I can start a major new trend in that."

Kamil lets out a wail from his highchair and Diana lifts her head hurriedly, the newspaper sticking to her in her haste. Kamil stops wailing and chuckles as Diana peels the paper from her head.

"You think that's funny do you?"

Kamil beams as Diana makes her way over to the highchair and picks him up.

"I think you need a bath little man."

Handing Kamil over to the nanny, Diana takes herself to the bedroom and wanders over to the phone. Picking it up, she dials without hesitation. The phone rings twice before he answers

"Hello?"

Diana speaks softly

"I've got some time free today. Can we meet?"
"Usual place, usual time?"

The man's voice is eager, his desire to see Diana apparent
"Kamil is with the nanny until four thirty, so I can only spare a few hours."
"I look forward to it."

Diana hangs up the phone without responding and makes her way into the bathroom with a hint of a smile on her face. Humming to herself she begins to move around the room, picking up a brush and running it through her short blonde hair before making her way into the bathroom. Staring in the mirror, Diana pulls slowly against her porcelain skin, tightening it into a false looking mask before releasing it back to its normal state. Switching the shower on, she lets it run and steam fills the room before undressing and stepping into the cubicle. The water washes over her and Diana closes her eyes and stands perfectly still for several minutes. Reaching out to the expensive bottles stored neatly beside the shower, she takes time over shampooing and conditioning her hair and washes her body several times before finally turning the water off and leaving the cubicle. Unable to see in the fogged up mirror, Diana wraps herself in a large creamy coloured towel and scoops up several tubs of rich moisturiser before making her way to the bedroom. Sitting herself in front of her vanity table, Diana begins slowly and meticulously moisturising every inch of her body, starting with her feet and working her way up. When she reaches her neck, Diana switches product for a smaller, more delicate tub, staring at the wording on the side before unscrewing the lid and taking a large scoop from the full pot. She massages the cream into her skin, closing her eyes and relaxing back into her chair as she does so. When she has finished with the moisturiser, Diana takes out her hairdryer and takes time to dry her hair, working slowly with the aid of several lotions, potions and gels and a small round brush. When her hair is completely dry Diana examines her reflection form several angles, taking a comb to several areas in her quest for perfection. Closing her eyes, she sprays hairspray in a heavy mist across her head, sealing her style and spluttering twice as the fog enters her mouth. Working slowly to apply her makeup, she aims for a minimal look, being careful to choose muted, natural colours and emphasising her natural beauty. When she has finished her blue eyes sparkle, framed by long lashes, and her skin looks dewy and radiant. Checking out her reflection, Diana seems unable to help the small, smug smile that settles on her face. After several minutes examining herself from every angle, she stands up and tucks her towel tighter around her body, before making her way to her walk- in wardrobe. Flinging the doors open, she examines the racks and rails of clothes laid out in front of her with a confused look on her face. Stepping forward gingerly, she runs her hands across the rail jam packed with expensive, multi coloured ball gowns wistfully. Heading towards the back of the room, Diana picks out an expensive pair of blue jeans and a simple white T-shirt. Backing out of the wardrobe, she grabs hold of a well tailored navy blue blazer as an afterthought and steps back into the bedroom.

A pile of clothes litter the bedroom floor, Diana steps over the discarded items and makes her way back into the closet, returning with a patterned dress. Looking out of the window, she takes in the grey skies and heavy clouds and does not even bother to try it on. Dropping it on to the growing pile on the floor, she returns to the wardrobe and begins rummaging again.

Diana stares at her reflection in the full length mirror, turning from side to side to get a complete idea of how her outfit looks. Frowning slightly, she turns a complete circle before picking up a long coat that completely covers what she is wearing. Throwing the coat on, she steps closer to the mirror to examine her hair and makeup. She wipes at a barely discernable smudge of eyeliner and fusses with her already perfect hair, before stepping back to admire her handiwork. Grimacing, Diana turns away from the mirror and picks up her handbag, deliberately avoiding seeing her reflection again as she leaves the room.

Picking up Kamil, she holds him close to her smiling warmly at his playful gurgles and chatter. Kissing the top of his head, Diana hands him back to the waiting nanny with a smile

"Now you be good little man, no getting up to any mischief."

Kamil squirms and reaches out back for her from the nannies arms.

"I'll be back later sweetheart. I love you."

Diana turns and makes her way to the front door as Kamil lets out an ear splitting wail. Looking over her shoulder, she can see his face red and his arms still reaching out for her. Diana turns and looks away quickly, hurrying towards the door and taking herself out of his sight. Waiting out in the hallway, Diana listens as his cries slowly subside, the nanny distracting him with toys until he is once again gurgling happily. Moving slowly, Diana walks towards the front door, looking back over her shoulder several times as if she expects to hear Kamil cry again. Reaching the door, she pauses for several minutes as if unsure what to do, before reaching out and opening it slowly. The cold air rushes into the hallway and Diana once again stops and listens for Kamil. Hearing nothing, she steps outside and closes the door firmly behind her, making her way down to the black four by four waiting in the driveway. She half smiles as the driver holds the door open for her and steps into the luxurious interior. Sinking down onto the leather seats, Diana straps herself in firmly and holds tight to the seat. The driver begins making a thorough check of the car, checking underneath and around all of the tyres before getting into the front seat. While he does this Diana stares forlornly at the front door of the house, almost as if she expects it to open. She is jolted out of her reverie when the driver lets himself into the car and starts the engine.

"Usual place?"

Shocked by the familiar phrase, Diana stares blankly at the driver for several seconds before bursting into tears, her carefully applied makeup running down her cheeks.

CHAPTER TWENTY NINE

Diana sits cross legged on the floor in the living room, surrounded by toys. She had been playing happily with Kamil for the best part of an hour, until Dodi's family had arrived. Now she sits abandoned on her own as the relatives rally around the small boy. The family visits have become a key part of the week, almost like any other normal family. Once a week, Dodi's father and various other close relations or friends, descend on the house, staying for dinner and to spend some time with Kamil. This particular afternoon Diana looks worn out and dejected, but her tired eyes and slump go unnoticed as the family witness Kamil walking for the first time. A little over a year old, they marvel at his shaky attempts to toddle across the room, his gaze firmly fixed on his mother. However, he only makes it a few steps before he is scooped up by his grandfather, Mohammad Al Fayed. He squeezes Kamil close to him, oblivious to the boys obvious discomfort. Diana watches in silence as her son is fussed over

"Such a clever boy. You are just like your father was at this age."

Mohammad beams at his grandson, who squirms harder and pulls a most unattractive face. Mohammad chuckles and sets the boy back on the floor, facing away from Diana. Kamil struggles to his feet and searches around him, a panicked look on his face.

"Mummy is right here darling."

Diana pipes up from the corner and the fussing family members look over to her as if they had forgotten she was there. Kamil beams at his mother, before he is scooped up again. Diana looks down to the floor and begins fussing with a thread of the carpet, looking up from time to time to see what Kamil is up to. The boy is taking wobbly steps from person to person, smiling and laughing with each of them, seemingly too involved in his new game to remember the quest for his mother. A shadow falls over Diana and she looks up to see Dodi standing over her. He speaks in a voice little more than a hiss

"What's the matter with you? The least you could do is pretend to be interested when my family are here."

Diana does not bother to respond, instead pulling herself into a standing position and staring at Dodi for a moment. Their noses are only millimetres apart and Diana holds the pose for several seconds before turning and walking out of the room, with one last glace to Kamil. Their standoff unnoticed by the rest of the family, Dodi waits for a second after Diana has left, before turning and immersing himself into the middle of the circle and scooping up Kamil, blowing raspberries on the boys stomach and smiling widely at his deep chuckles. Diana waits outside in the hallway, listening to the conversation intently as if unsure that she will not be missed. After several minutes she turns and walks up the stairs, no one apart from Dodi even aware that she has gone.

Diana sits alone in the bedroom, spread out across the bed and stares at the phone. She makes no move to pick up the receiver or dial any numbers, but focuses with such intensity it seems she is trying to make it ring of its own accord. When, after around fifteen minutes, nothing has happened, Diana gets up off of the bed and slips quietly to the bedroom door. Cracking it open just a bit, she listens to the sounds of joviality coming from downstairs. Pulling the door further open, Diana slips right out into the hall and concentrates on the noise floating up to her. After several seconds a puzzled look flashes across her face and she edges closer to the top of the stairs and resumes listening. A look of comprehension crosses her face and she frowns, before heading back into the bedroom and slamming the door behind her, muttering to herself

"They wait until I'm out of the room and they drop the pretence completely. Now I've gone they're not even bothering to speak English. God knows what they do with Kamil while they're at the mosque. It's like I'm not even a consideration. Who cares what I think, what I want. I'm only his mother!"

Diana throws herself back on to the bed dejectedly and buries her face in the covers. So absorbed by her own musings she does not hear the bedroom door open quietly.

"So this is where you're hiding yourself."

There is no hint of humour in Dodi's voice, his tone low and angry. Diana does not look up, ignoring the comment. When Dodi speaks again his voice is clouded with temper and shakes as if he is doing his best not to shout

"Is it too much to ask that when my family are here you conduct yourself with a little bit of decorum? You're always sullen and withdrawn, but disappearing while we have guests is a whole new low for you."

Diana props herself up on her elbows and looks at Dodi sadly, her blue eyes glassy with unshed tears
"I didn't think I'd be missed."

Her voice is low and shaky like Dodi's, but seems to be more in an attempt to keep her tears in check. Dodi's voice is louder as he responds
"Oh don't be so ridiculous Diana. I should have known you'd do something absurd like lock yourself away just because you're not the centre of attention."

Diana pulls herself up into a sitting position
"It's not that I'm not the centre of attention, it's because it's like I'm not even there. As soon as your family turn up, every single week, I don't even get a look in. I listened to you all with Kamil, as soon as I'm out the door you don't even bother to speak English to him anymore. How else am I supposed to feel except shoved aside?"
"You know it's not like that. Am I supposed to keep Kamil away from his heritage just because it upsets you?"

Diana looks hurt
"I don't even know why I bother to talk to you Dodi, you don't understand me at all. You completely fail to see my point of view. It's all about you and what you want and what you think is best. At some point you are going to have to realise that you can't be right one hundred percent of the time."

Diana stands up and makes her way out of the room, walking down the stairs and straight into the living room where Dodi's family are still gathered. Without looking at, or speaking to, anyone there, she scoops up Kamil and struts out from the room. Dodi, who is making his way down the stairs, is just in time to see Diana pick up Kamil's coat and changing bag and head out of the door. He looks to the living room, where his family have gathered around the doorway to watch Diana leave and shrugs his shoulders apologetically, before following after her. As he reaches the front door he sees the standard black four by four pulling away from the house. Kamil, strapped tightly in his mother's lap, has a confused look on his face and begins to cry as the car speeds away from his waiting father and the family members who have gathered around Dodi.

Diana looks down at Kamil in her lap, his face scrunched up and red and his screams ripping through the car. Even the driver, usually professional in every sense, can't help wincing with each new shriek. Diana bounces her knee gently and makes shushing noises to him, but Kamil pays no attention. Already pale and stressed out, Diana holds the boy close to her despite his resistance and speaks soothing words

"Come on now darling, we're just going out in the car for a little bit. Just you and me. Won't that be nice? No need for all these tears, we're just getting a little bit of time together. We're going to have lots of fun."

The driver continues to shoot concerned looks to the back of the car, even as Kamil's tantrum wears down. Diana, who has forsaken her usual firm grip on the seat so that she can hold on to her son, looks tense and worn out and her eyes keep flickering to Kamil as if she is sure he is about to start screaming again. Exhausted from his temper tantrum, Kamil's eyes begin to get heavy, lulled by the movement of the car and soon his head is pressed close to his mothers chest and his eyes are firmly closed. Diana watches him for a few moments, before the gentle movement of the car and her own exhaustion finally catch up with her and she too dozes off. Having given no destination to the driver at the start of the journey, he wavers at a junction, before deciding to head out of the city and away from the stress and noise of London.

Diana wakes up and looks down at Kamil, still asleep against her chest. The single seatbelt is strapped across the two of them and Diana smiles down at her sleeping son. Tucking one hand gently around Kamil, she stretches her back before undoing the belt and letting it reel back into its holder. Outside of the car the sky is darkening and clouds hang heavy and low with the promise of rain at the least, if not snow. Diana looks to the driver, still sitting in the front seat and avoiding her penetrative gaze uncomfortably.

"Where are we?"

As Diana waits for a reply she looks out of the window at the grassy landscape surrounding them, taking in several stables and large paddocks in the distance. The driver shifts in his seat and does not look at Diana as he responds

"You only told me to drive, you fell asleep before you said where you wanted to go."

There is a hint of defiance in his tone and his cheeks colour red as he speaks. Diana stares at him and waits for him to speak again. He clears his throat

"You've been coming here a lot recently and I thought it might do you good to get out of London. You clearly needed rest and it's so noisy and stressful in the city that I thought getting out into the country might be the best thing."

His voice trails off as he looks into the rear view mirror and catches sight of the look on Diana's face. Diana, who has flushed deep red, looks down to Kamil who is stirring in her arms and responds in a small voice

"Just take us home, please."

Dodi is pacing the living room when Diana and Kamil make their way quietly back into the house. Although only late afternoon, the sky is almost black and inside the house it appears as dark as night. Dodi rushes out into the hall as soon as he hears the front door close with a quiet click. He looks to Kamil, who Diana has placed on the floor between herself and Dodi, before speaking in a carefully controlled voice

"Where have you been?"

Diana looks embarrassed and avoids the question

"I'm so sorry about the way I behaved. I was completely out of line. Were your family very upset?"

Dodi stares at her for a moment, deflated as if he had been spoiling for a fight. He scoops up Kamil in his arms

"They were confused mostly, but I explained that Kamil had an appointment with the doctor that you had forgotten about and that you must have been so keen not to miss it that you obviously didn't remember to say goodbye."

Dodi looks Diana in the eye who blushes and responds in a soft voice.

"Thank you. I'll apologise myself when we see them next."

Dodi fusses over Kamil, not looking at Diana as he replies quietly

"I don't like lying for you, especially not to my family."

Diana walks towards Dodi and Kamil and attempts to wrap her arms around the pair of them. Kamil gurgles happily, wriggling in his father's arms

"You won't have to again. I promise."

CHAPTER THIRTY

Diana relaxes on the bench and watches William and Harry help Kamil up on to the climbing frame. Together the three boys laugh, William especially taking extra care of his baby brother. The three boys, all so different in looks, play together happily. Diana smiles and closes her eyes briefly, leaning back on the bench and relaxing her posture as she reopens her eyes and watches the boys. Harry runs up to the bench at top speed, panting as he flops down next to his mother.

"Can we go for something to eat soon?"

Diana wraps her arm around Harry and leans her fair head against his coppery one.

"Of course we can, are you hungry?"

Harry nods enthusiastically, his gaze now taken with William and Kamil who are playing an enthusiastic game of chase across the grass. Harry looks wistfully towards Kamil, before turning to his mother.

"It's nice not being the baby any more, but sometimes I do miss it."

Diana pulls Harry closer to her and kisses the top of his head

"You'll always be a baby to me."

Harry opens his mouth as if to say something, before thinking better of it and closing it again. He sits in silence for several minutes, watching William and Kamil.

"Is everything alright?"

Diana and Harry ask the question at exactly the same moment and they turn to each other and laugh before a sombre look crosses Diana's face

"Of course. Everything is fine. What would make you ask that?"

Harry looks uncomfortable and Diana wraps her arm tighter around him

"You can talk to me Harry, it's alright."

Harry does not look up and rubs his shoes together as he speaks

"It's about Camilla."

His voice trails off as a clouded look crosses Diana's face. He begins to push himself off of the bench

"Never mind. It's not important."

Diana takes hold of his arm a little more forcefully than necessary and Harry winces and she promptly lets go.

"I'm sorry, but Harry, if it's important enough to have you worried then it's important enough for me to want to hear about. Sit down and we'll talk together."

Harry reluctantly places himself back on the bench, sitting further away from his mother than he was previously and looks down at the ground. Diana's tone is encouraging and she reaches out and takes hold of his hand as she speaks

"You said something about Camilla?"

Diana's face is carefully impassive and she looks to Harry, waiting for him to speak again.

"She said that there was something wrong with you. That you needed to see someone. Are you sick?"

Harry looks up and into his mothers eyes with concern as the last words tumble from his mouth as if by accident. Diana breathes deeply, as if trying to keep her temper in check, before responding.

"I'm fine. Maybe Camilla just got the wrong end of the stick. Are you sure she was talking about me?"

Harry nods.

"I don't think she meant me to hear. She was talking on the phone and saying something about how she thinks that you've been acting odd recently and that in her opinion you needed some help. Then she mentioned something about a hospital and I thought you might be sick."

Harry's face takes on a pained look and he stares at his mother waiting for reassurance. Diana, whose face has turned from pasty white to deep crimson, takes several moments to answer.

"I....I don't know why she would say something like that Harry. I promise you it's most certainly not true."

Harry avoids his mothers gaze, instead looking at his shoes as Diana continues

"Have you been spending a lot of time with Camilla recently?"

Her tone is guarded, full of clearly feigned nonchalance. She tries to make her question sound casual, and as if she would be completely indifferent regardless of Harry's answer.

"Yeah, quite a lot. She's there pretty much all of the time. Sometimes we go out together."

Harry's tone is almost identical to his mothers, although filled with sincerity. Diana's face slowly seeps back to a pasty white colour and her eyes take on a glassy look.

"Oh. Well, that's nice I suppose. Where do you go?"

Harry is tracing the tip of his expensive shoes through the dirt, making patterns, and does not look up to answer his mother

"Just out. Sometimes she takes us to school, or helps with our homework."

Enthralled with his dirt drawing, Harry does not see his mother's eyes fill with tears. Before they can spill over, William comes running over to the bench, a crying Kamil hoisted over his shoulder. His breath comes out in short pants

"He fell over. On his knee. Can't see any blood but I couldn't calm him down. Is he going to be ok?"

William had not noticed his mother's face in his haste to pass Kamil over to her and once Diana had the boy in her arms she seemed completely absorbed in her concern for him. Checking him all over, she looks up to William and releases a smile of pure relief

"He's fine. Probably just tired I think. It's hard work playing with big boys all afternoon."

Diana smiles down at Kamil, who had settled almost as soon as he felt her arms wrap around him. William looks slightly pacified

"So he's alright? And I didn't do anything wrong?"

Diana reaches out and pulls her eldest son into a tight embrace

"Of course you didn't do anything wrong. Boys get into scrapes all the time, no matter how old they are. The only difference is that the little ones don't mind their Mummy seeing that they cry about it."

Diana laughs as she speaks and presses her nose to Kamil's, who laughs happily in response. William heaves a sigh of relief and a warm smile spreads across his whole face when Kamil turns to face him and offers a gummy grin in his direction. Diana laughs

"Time to feed the troops I think. Who's hungry?"

Kamil squeals and throws his hands up in the air as the older boys chorus their approval and Diana laughs softly. She reaches out to pull them all into a tight embrace before releasing William and Harry and they begin to make their way towards the waiting car.

Diana shifts uncomfortably in her seat and stares around the room, taking in the people around them. The pizzeria that William and Harry had begged to be allowed to eat in is heaving, families packed around the small tables taking advantage of a low cost meal. Diana looks to William and Harry, who are helping to strap

Kamil into his highchair and struggling to get his legs into the right holes. Kamil is giggling happily, waving around a fork that he has grabbed from one of the tables on his way past.

"Did we have to come here?"

William and Harry look at their mother, both faces twins of incredulity

"You said that we could have pizza."

Diana nods once

"Yes, but I thought we'd go to a quiet Italian restaurant somewhere up town. Somewhere a bit less....crowded."

Diana chooses her last word carefully, but her point doesn't go unnoticed by the two boys. Finally managing to strap their brother into his seat, the two elder boys take a seat either side of their mother.

"We hardly ever get to come to places like these."

William begins and Harry chips in

"Normal places. Places that people our age like to go."

The wounded faces on each of the boys, so clearly put on, makes Diana laugh and she concedes

"OK, well I suppose we're here now anyway. Let's order some food."

As if by magic a waitress appears at the side of the table, pen and notepad in her hands. She does not look up as she speaks

"Are you ready to order?"

As Diana begins to list things from the menu the waitress looks up to her customer. Short and squat, the young woman stares open mouthed at the people seated at the table in front of her. William and Harry look at each other and stifle giggles. Completely oblivious, Diana keeps talking to the woman who has frozen in front of her. Diana looks up

"Did you get all of that? Oh and can we have some soft drinks and a jug of water for the table please?"

She stares expectantly at the woman who has yet to put pen to paper. Diana looks to the boys, Kamil bashing away happily on the tray of the highchair, and then back to the waitress.

"Excuse me?"

The woman seems to snap out of her reverie and blushes furiously

"You're....."

Diana seems to be losing her patience.

"I know quite well who we all are thank you, what I'd like to do is order some food."

Blushing an even deeper shade of red, the woman holds up her pad and paper and begins taking notes as Diana goes through their order again. She sighs theatrically as the young woman hurries from the table and towards the kitchen to deposit their order. At the table across, a woman turns round and stares at their table for several seconds, before turning back to her husband and talking furiously. Two children sit either side of the man and woman, unmindful of their parents conversation. Diana, facing out across the room, does a quick scan, before focusing intently on her family around her. She looks to William, feigning nonchalance

"So, Harry mentioned that you've been out and about with Camilla a lot recently."

Diana picks up her fork and twiddles it absentmindedly on the stained white tablecloth. William shoots a dirty look to Harry, who shrugs in response, before replying

"Well, a little bit. I suppose. Not that much."

Diana does not look at him, but instead focuses all her attention on wiping a tiny smear of dribble from Kamil's chin, who smiles happily at her in response.

"Do you like spending time with her?"

William looks confused, as if he does not know the right way to answer the question, and hesitates before speaking

"I, um, don't mind it."

He shrugs his shoulders in an exaggerated motion as Diana suddenly focuses her gaze on him, her intense blue eyes clear and questioning. She holds his gaze for several seconds before drinks are deposited on the table in front of her. The waitress, a different one from the one who took their order, begins to babble at her

"Your food won't be long. I hope you don't mind me saying, but you're a wonderful inspiration. My friend Donna has gone all spiritual because of you. It's done her the world of good, if you don't mind me saying, she was a bit of a lost cause before, but she's turned it all around because of you. I've been thinking that I might follow in her, well yours really, footsteps. You know, start looking at religion a bit more seriously. What do you think I should do?"

She looks intently at Diana, who stares at her blankly until she begins to back away from the table. William and Harry glance at each other but do not say anything to their mother. Before normal conversation can start, the woman from the table across has got up from the seat and approached Diana and the boys

"Excuse me, I hope you don't mind me coming over. I thought it was you, such an honour to meet you, and here of all places."

The woman lets out a high pitched giggle and Diana frowns slightly at her

"Anyway, I wanted to come over to tell you that I'm all for what you're doing, turning Muslim and all that. A woman should be able to follow her heart, wherever it takes her and I think that......"

Diana cuts her off sharply

"If you don't mind, we'd like to eat our dinner in peace."

Diana's tone is curt and the woman looks offended and moves back to her table. William and Harry stare at their mother, who is saved from explaining her behaviour by the arrival of their food. The boys tuck in hungrily to the pizza, with even Kamil gnawing happily away. Diana picks at her food, barely touching the one piece of Pizza she helped herself to. When the waitress comes to clear away their food, Diana nods distractedly when asked if she has finished and barely seems to notice when her plate is cleared away.

CHAPTER THIRTY ONE

Diana sits on her bed, listening to the phone ring. She makes no move to answer it, just stares at the handset until the noise stops. Sighing, she counts silently to ten before the noise starts again. Diana leans back on her bed and covers her head with the pillow until the ringing stops. Then starts again. At the stroke of ten pm the phone stops ringing for the last time and Diana removes the pillow from her head and listens for the front door slamming to signal that Dodi has arrived home. His muted footsteps plod rhythmically up the stairs, stopping first at Kamil's room. It is his first port of call every time he returns home, regardless of the time. Diana slips silently off of the bed and treads slowly in her bare feet out of the room. She pads softly to Kamil's room, clearing her throat softly as she enters, alerting Dodi to her presence. He does not turn around and Diana slides her arms around his torso and leans the side of her head on to his back. They stay like this for several moments, Dodi staring down at Kamil fast asleep in his cot.

"He'll need to go into a bed soon. He's getting so big."

Wistfully Dodi reaches down and strokes a lock of dark hair from out of Kamil's eyes. The boy stirs, stretching his hands above his head, before settling back down.

"I don't know where the time's gone."

Dodi is speaking softly, his words seeming to be more for his own benefit than for Diana's.

"It's been a difficult few years."

Diana's voice is low, her words halting. After a moment she adds

"I wouldn't change anything though."

Dodi turns smoothly, placing his back to Kamil but keeping Diana's arms wrapped around him. He looks down at her, taking in her pale face and the shadows under her eyes. Without speaking he wraps his arms around her waist and pulls her close to him so that she can rest her head on his chest. The room is heavy with silence, the only noise the deep rhythm of Kamil's breathing. Diana doesn't even seem to have realised that she had been crying noiseless tears until she notices that Dodi's shirt is wet. She removes herself from their embrace and takes Dodi's hand

"Come on, let's get you changed and into bed."

Diana and Dodi lay side by side in bed, each turned to face each other. Neither of them speak for several moments, until Diana reaches out to take Dodi's hand underneath the covers.

"I'm sorry."

Dodi looks confused and waits for Diana to elaborate.

"I know things have been....."

She grasps around for the right word

"Difficult."

Comprehension dawns on Dodi's face but before he can speak Diana continues. Her words come out in a rush as if she is keen to be rid of them

"I also know that I haven't helped. I've probably made things worse. But I promise from now on that I'm going to try harder to make things as simple as possible. Our life is complicated enough without me adding to it, I know that now."

Dodi nods his head slowly, as if he is trying to wrap his head around her words

"It's not just my fault though. It takes two people to argue, two people not to get on. And in our case it's been even more than that."

Dodi looks confused before a look of suspicion crosses his face. Diana reddens but adds hurriedly

"I meant your family. They're constantly here Dodi and I feel like they're judging me all of the time. Putting pressure on me to convert and making me feel like I'm not good enough for you, not good enough to be Kamil's mother if I don't."

Dodi looks hurt

"That's not fair Diana. You know how close I am to my family and they've never been anything but welcoming towards you. My father especially. And like me, all they want for Kamil is the best."

"I'm just trying to tell you how I feel Dodi. I want us both to get everything out in the open so that we can fix things. There has been such a distance between us lately and I don't want things to be like that."

Diana shuffles closer to Dodi under the covers so that their bodies are practically touching and looks up at Dodi imploringly. He sighs softly before wrapping his arms around her.

"No more fighting? We both say whatever we need to right now, with no arguments and we'll each work on what the other one has to say?"

Diana nods once and locks her eyes with Dodi's dark ones. He takes a deep breath

"I'm disappointed that you haven't converted to Islam."

He lets the statement hang in the air for several seconds, before continuing softly

"I never really thought about it until you were expecting Kamil, but once you started going to the mosque I was thrilled. I thought it could be something that we could do as a family, time we could share together. And you seemed so peaceful and interested at the beginning. And when your interest trailed off I couldn't help but be disappointed. I thought that it could be so good for you, for all of us. I don't like thinking about you all on your own while I take Kamil to the mosque with my family. You are my family too, our family, and it doesn't feel right that you're not a part of it."

Diana breathes deeply

"I didn't realise that you felt that way. I thought it was all about me not being good enough, not being the right type of woman. The right type of mother."

Dodi looks shocked

"How could you possibly think that? You know that I love you. How could someone that I love not be the right sort of woman? How could someone as amazing as you are with Kamil not be the right sort of mother?"

Diana stares at Dodi, her mouth open as if she is struggling to find the right words to say. Dodi continues

"Diana, I'm not the sort of man that would propose to a woman that I didn't want to be with. I wouldn't have been so pleased that you were pregnant if I didn't think you were the 'right sort of woman'. Where have you got that notion from anyway?"

Diana blushes and mutters something too low for Dodi to hear. He looks confused for a second before comprehension dawns on his face.

"The news. Of course. I thought you'd been in the spotlight long enough to ignore whatever lies the media chooses to spread?"

Diana looks down, avoiding Dodi's gaze

"Mostly I do. But this time it wasn't just things that the media had dreamed up all on their own, well not all of it anyway. People in the Muslim community actually protested against me converting. You got letters advising you not to be with me."

Dodi looks confused and guilty at the same time and Diana offers by way of explanation

"I found a letter in your suit pocket. I presume it wasn't the only one you got?"

This time it is Dodi who is avoiding Diana's gaze, his cheeks flushing before he finally looks up at her. His eyes are hard

"I didn't listen though. How many times at the beginning of our relationship did we tell each other that this was just about us and the way we felt? It has nothing to do with what anyone else thinks or feels. I mean, I presume Charles had something to say about your relationship with me?"

Diana flushes crimson but stares right back at Dodi

"Of course he did. We knew he would."

"But you chose to keep it from me. Presumably to spare my feelings, like I tried to do for you."

They stare at each other, practically nose to nose and Diana's eyes fill with tears. Dodi speaks softly, reaching out to wipe away the one tear that slips down her cheek

"We were both trying to do the right thing for each other, we just went about it the wrong way. Maybe if we were a bit more open with each other from the beginning we wouldn't be going through this right now."

Diana nods her agreement, before adding

"Well, we know now. We know we have to trust and depend on each other, be there for each other and listen to each other. We know that we need to start making more of an effort."

Dodi smiles widely, his hand still resting on the side of Diana's face. She smiles back, pressing her cheek into his hand affectionately.

"We can do this, can't we?"

Diana's words are soft but there is hope in her blue eyes. Dodi looks down at her and smiles.

"We can do anything."

Chapter Thirty Two

I couldn't believe it at the time, but now that it's had a while to sink in I'm starting to wonder how I ever thought it would be any different. I mean, I suppose parts of it seemed to make sense, in some ways it was like any other relationship. Girl meets boy. Girl likes boy. Girl flirts excessively and converts religion to appeal to boy. Well, maybe that bit isn't so traditional.

That afternoon at the Mosque everyone continued to whisper and point and gossip. I figured that the safest thing to do would be stick as close to Arun as possible and that way we'd get through it together. Apparently I was wrong. And so was he when he told me that it didn't matter what anyone else thought. He told me later that he had actually believed that everything would be all right and that even if people did have a problem with us as a couple then they'd soon get over it. I guess it might have happened that way too, if the Imam hadn't got involved. What did our relationship have to do with him anyway? When I found out that he'd told Arun that he couldn't be with me I was furious and stormed back to the mosque to confront him. Apparently though, this only lent weight to his argument that I wasn't the right sort of woman to be with a Muslim man. It was perfectly acceptable, welcomed even, that I converted because then I would be leading a better and more spiritual life. But I could never be good enough to be with a Muslim man, unless I found another convert like myself. Those were his actual words. That, and something about me being too westernised, not chaste enough. Basically calling me a slut. And then he had the cheek to ask about the physical side of mine and Arun's relationship, like that had anything to do with him. I stormed off at that point, not wanting to say something in temper that I would regret later. Not that it helped with Arun. The damage was already done there. He said that my outburst certainly hadn't done me any favours but that his mind was already made up before I'd said anything. What sort of man allows anyone to tell him how he's allowed to feel, who he's supposed to fall in love with? All right, we hadn't exactly said that we were in love yet, but I'm sure we were on the brink of it, until all of this.

At first I'd just been too stunned to say anything. Then the waterworks started. I didn't beg though, so at least I've still got that part of my dignity. For what it's worth. I foolishly believed that when he came round to see me he was going to apologise for being so distant at the Mosque and that we would talk and laugh about everything that was said and agree that we would get through it together. When he turned up at my flat he was still distant, but I wanted to pretend that he just had things on his mind so I made him a cup of tea and waited for him to talk to me. When he didn't, I kissed him and he kissed me back. Forcefully. And then we were on the floor in the living room with no clothes on. I'm not really sure how it happened, all I can remember at the time was thinking how lucky it is that I live alone and that no one could walk in and see us at it. Pretty much as soon as we were done Arun got dressed and left. He kissed me goodbye and promised to call me but he couldn't look at me. I knew then what he was going to do and I was so mad about it. So mad that he would bend to the pressure and just give up because a couple of people disapproved. So mad that he could come to my home and sleep with me knowing that he was planning on breaking up with me. So mad that he clearly didn't have the guts to tell me to my face.

I still couldn't help but cry when he did call, three days later. I'd promised myself that I wouldn't. That I was strong enough to stand up to him and tell him just how pathetic I thought he was, and that I didn't need someone like that in my life anyway. I like to think I would have done it too, if he hadn't started crying first. I felt so bad for him and everything started to look different when I realised that we were both hurting so much about it. It felt a bit like Romeo and Juliet, only it wasn't a family feud keeping us apart, but religion. Although I suppose in some ways it is almost like a family. So then I started crying, telling him that I understood why we had to end things and that I was still planning on coming to the same mosque and wasn't it better that we stayed friends seeing as we would still have to see each other. His crying stopped as soon as I started being understanding. Once I'd said that I understood we were breaking up he couldn't get off of the phone quick enough. Said he had somewhere to be, that his parents were expecting him or something and then the line went dead in my hand. For a moment I was so shocked I just stood there holding the phone in my hand like a complete moron, until it dawned on me. He wasn't sorry, he'd just sounded upset so that I'd go easy on him. So that I'd do all the hard work. I'd broken up with the man I loved because his *family* had managed to convince both of us that I wasn't good enough for him.

I haven't been to uni since it all happened. There is no way that I could face Jameela after everything that went on. She's bound to know all about it, because that's what it's like. Everyone knows everyone else's business. I tried calling her after that first day at the mosque, the day where everything started to fall apart. I was going to apologise for not telling her. And if I'm honest, I was hoping for a bit of a shoulder to cry on. To have someone to talk to about what a horrible day it had been and have her tell me that it would all blow over. I would have felt so much better to hear it from someone who had been there that it wasn't as bad as I thought it had been, that people would soon think nothing of it. She answered the phone and I think at first she didn't realise that it was me. Probably due to all the crying I had been doing. I doubt if she'd seen me she would have recognised me either, what with the lack of makeup, red eyes and snotty nose. Anyway, so I managed to splutter out her name and ask how she was before she twigged who was on the phone and suddenly she starts saying that Jameela wasn't in or couldn't come to the phone right now or something like that. Like I didn't realise that it was her. I just hung up after that. I figured that if that was her attitude, my so called friend, then everyone else's would be pretty much the same. If even my friend didn't want to talk to me, just for being in a relationship, then I doubt very much that anyone else will start being more accepting anytime soon. I called my mum after that, and sobbed down the phone at her. It wasn't the first time I'd cried to her about a boy though, and it probably won't be the last. I don't think she really understood how hurt I was, how hard it had been to have everyone judging me and finding me lacking. She kept saying things like 'there's plenty more fish in the sea' and 'you've got to kiss a few frogs before you find your prince.' I hung up on her too, after that, and just sat by myself having a good cry. Sometimes it makes you feel better, but all it did this time is make me feel a hundred times worse. By the time I was all cried out I had a pounding headache and my face was all red and blotchy. I stared at the phone for a while, hoping that my Arun, or even my mum or Jameela would ring. After that I sat and stared at the door for a while, figuring that Arun was more likely to just turn up. Trying to convince myself that, like before, he'd know how upset I was and just turn up on my doorstep to make it all better. I don't know what time I fell asleep waiting, but when I woke curled up on the sofa in the early hours, the door and the phone were still as silent as ever.

Needless to say I haven't been back to the mosque. I can imagine what people are saying. That I only went there because of Diana, that I only stayed because of Arun. I'd like to prove them wrong but I'm just not strong enough to face going back. To face all their condescending looks. To spend time with them all now I know what they really think about me. I tried looking over some of the stuff that Arun had showed me; I thought it might make me feel better. Make me realise that it wasn't all about him. The problem was that all I could think about when I was looking at it was him, and having my lessons with him and how it all made more sense when he was explaining it to me. I've had a couple of phone calls from uni this last week, asking if I was ok. I explained that I hadn't been well and they couldn't have been nicer. Except for the fact that I'll probably have to defer because I've missed so much. If things were different that would have been something that I would have spoken to Arun about, because he would have sat down and been able to convince me that I could do it. But things aren't different. And I've tried calling him a few times over the last few weeks, the last few months. He always gets his mum or his dad to tell me that he isn't home. I can tell that they're lying though because I can always hear him whispering in the background. Once I even heard his mum call out to him while his dad was busy telling me that he'd gone out. The last time that I'd phoned they weren't so nice. Told me to stop calling or they would report me to the police. I never wanted things to turn out this way, all I did was fall in love. I've decided that I'll have to go to the mosque to talk to him, regardless of what anyone has to say about it. I need to get my point across. I need to find out why he changed his mind after everything he promised me.

I need to tell him that I'm pregnant.

Chapter Thirty Three

Diana walks slowly up the aisle of the deserted church, running one hand softly along the polished wooden pews on her left. Her footsteps echo off of the flagstones on the floor and up into the high slanted roof. On her right hand side the late summer sun filters through the stained glass windows, sending different colours down on to the floor to line her path ahead. Choosing seemingly at random, Diana slips into one of the pews and settles down on to the hard wooden bench. The old wood groans quietly at the contact and the sound echoes through the church. In front of Diana the lectern stands high, an eagle carved ornately into the wood. Behind that, the space for the choir lay empty, the alter with the image of Christ hanging above it looks bare. Diana leans forward and presses her head softly against the polished wood of the pew in front of her. She inhales deeply and smiles to herself as a beam of sunlight shines down through one of the stained glass windows and on to her back. On a tiny shelf on the back of each pew a bible and a hymn book are laid out, alternating in a pattern of dark brown and bottle green. Diana reaches out and picks up the hymn book, leafing through the delicate thin pages and staring intently at the miniscule print. Occasionally she smiles and begins humming a tune softly to herself, before turning the page again. Lost in her own thoughts, she does not hear the vicar approach her.

"May I help you, my dear? The next service isn't until much later this evening."

Diana looks up and smiles warmly at the man in front of her, who seems taken aback by her presence.
"Lady Diana. It's an honour to have you here."

Diana stands and embraces the man swiftly, before pulling away and looking embarrassed and straightening out the creases in his black gown and apologising
"I'm sorry, I was just passing and it's such a beautiful church I thought I'd drop in."

Diana looks pained
"If now isn't convenient then I can come back another time. Maybe for a service?"

Smiling, the vicar gestures to the pew and Diana sits down, sliding a long to make enough room for him to sit comfortably next to her
"Any time is the perfect time to come to church. That's why the doors are never locked. Well, in the day time at least. I would love to keep the doors unlocked all of the time, but unfortunately we don't live in that world anymore."

He looks morose for a moment, before seeming to remember where he is and offering Diana his hand
"Reverend Edwards."

Diana shakes his podgy hand politely before releasing it and gesturing to the stained glass windows
"They look so beautiful in this weather. They reminded me of the church that I used to go to whilst I was at school."

Reverend Edwards smiles and looks up to the windows
"They are stunning, especially when the sun catches the light like that."

He looks to Diana and smiles
"Lovely weather we've been having, long may it continue."

Diana seems puzzled by the sudden change in conversation and half smiles
"Don't you want to know why I'm here as opposed to....."

The sentence trails off and Reverend Edwards smiles at Diana warmly
"All that matters is that you are here. The why is irrelevant."

He reaches out and takes Diana's hand tentatively and looks up at her face, before speaking softly
"Although, I would assume that if you are here it is because there is something on your mind. Either that or you're looking for something."

He does not wait for Diana to respond, instead continuing
"It's always nice when anyone comes here, for any reason at all. Obviously we have dedicated people that turn up for every service. And then we have the once a weekers. And then the once a month or less. But it doesn't matter who you are, how often you come to church, if at all. Anyone who comes here for help,

guidance, advice or even just a little bit of time to think, is welcome."

Catching sight of Diana's smile at his last comment, the vicar smiles

"I see I've hit the nail on the head there. Well, I'll leave you to it. You don't need me babbling in your ear."

Diana begins to protest but he raises his hand to silence her

"I've got things that I really should be getting on with anyway. But you sit there as long as you need to and if you need me I'll not be too far away."

He stands up and moves lithely out from the pew, smiling down at Diana as he does so

"As I said earlier, the next service isn't until this evening. Feel free to have a wander about. There is a lovely little coffee morning going on in one of the Sunday school rooms, if you feel that you'd like to pop in."

He holds his hands out

"No pressure. But if you do need anything, I'll be around."

Diana smiles gratefully, keeping the smile locked firmly on her face until Reverend Edwards is out of her sight. Relaxing her posture into a slump, Diana's smile drops into a look of confusion. The hymn book that she abandoned earlier had fallen on to the floor, so Diana reaches down to retrieve it, knocking her head on the wooden pew in front of her. Seeming to forget where she is momentarily Diana swears loudly and rubs her forehead as she sits back up. Looking over both shoulders, Diana checks that no one is around before raising herself out her seat and shuffling along to the other end of the pew. Exiting back out on to the flagstone floor, Diana moves to take a closer look at some of the pictures on the glass, mesmerised by the bright colours and intricate detail.

The main doors to the church open and a young couple walk through, their hands tightly clasped. Through the open doors the sunlight illuminates the aisle that they are walking up. Cheerfully the woman turns to the man and points out the windows on either side of the church and how the colours reflect out on to the floor in front of them. Smiling, Diana slips behind one of the pillars supporting the church and watches as the man and the woman continue to walk forwards, pointing out pretty little details littered around the church. As if from nowhere, the vicar appears behind Diana, causing her to jump as he reaches out and touches her waist lightly. He points to the couple

"They're getting married. Never seen either of them here before, but it's still so nice that they want to get married in a church. So many people are opting for a registry office or some white sandy beach nowadays; it always makes me smile to think that there are still some youngsters who want to do things the traditional way."

Diana looks at the vicar in confusion

"Does it not seem a bit hypocritical to you that they only want to come here because they're getting married?"

Reverend Edwards smiles warmly

"I can see how it would upset some vicars, but to me it's a chance to bring people back into the flock. It's much the same with Christenings. I see so many parents who want me to baptise their child, despite the fact that I've never seen them at church. Still, to me, it's a chance for them to realise that they're missing out. Those few visits to a church can sometimes be enough to make people come back for good. And even if not, what kind of God would not want to share in some of the most joyous events in his children's life?"

Smiling, the vicar steps out from the pillar and waves to the couple, wrapping his arms warmly around the pair of them as he approaches. He guides them off towards the room he indicated to Diana earlier, offering them refreshments and a chance to talk about any questions they might have. As soon as their voices have gone, Diana steps out from her hiding place and wanders slowly off in the same direction. Pausing at the door, she listens to the voices wafting through a slight gap where the door has not closed properly.

"I've always dreamed of having a church wedding. I know we don't come as often as we should......"

The girls voice trails off, embarrassed and Diana listens harder at the door for the vicars response

"Of course we like to have the opportunity to get to know the people that we, as a church, will be marrying. Perhaps it wouldn't be too much to ask that you pop a long to a service or two before the actual ceremony."

Diana smiles at the vicars pleasant manner and the chorus of grateful agreement from the bride and groom. Slipping away from the door, she begins a slow wander around the church, taking time to run her fingers over intricate tapestries hanging on the walls and heavy brass figures dotted around. Lost in her own thoughts she does not notice the old woman who practically walks in to her in an attempt to get her attention

"Oh, I am sorry dear. I thought I heard someone walking around out here. I came to see if you wanted a cup of tea?"

The woman looks to Diana, the question etched on her face. Diana waits a few moments before responding, the woman staring at her intently

"That would be lovely, thank you."

Showing no signs of recognising Diana, the woman turns on her heels and begins heading back the way that she came, leaving Diana to follow after her

Five minutes later and fifty pence worse off, Diana sits down at a clean white table in the now deserted Sunday school and takes a sip of a lukewarm cup of tea the colour of dishwater. Diana smiles to herself as the elderly woman slides into the seat opposite her with surprising grace and sets down a plate of biscuits between them. Diana reaches out and takes a custard cream, dipping it once into her tea before taking a bite.

"I haven't seen you here before."

Still showing no sign of recognising Diana, the woman fishes for information crudely and Diana tries to hide her smile as she responds

"No, I was just passing by and thought I'd pop in and look around."

The woman eyes her suspiciously, as if not sure to believe her words

"We don't get a lot of people in here just looking around."

Diana ignores her and changes the subject
"I met Reverend Edwards, he seems nice."

The old woman's face lights up at the mention of the vicars name
"Oh yes, he's lovely. Really knows his stuff. Makes the services interesting, you know? The one that was here before him, well sometimes I'd find myself nodding off while he was talking, but not with Reverend Edwards. Helps that he's easy on the eye too."

The woman winks at Diana who almost chokes on her tea.
"I suppose it would."

Her tone is polite, a hint of laughter barely creeping through. If she notices, the woman does not mention it, instead continuing
"We don't get a lot of new people coming here. Mostly it's just the same people week in and week out. It's not fashionable, see. Terrible, if you ask me. Religion shouldn't be something that's done because it's trendy."

Diana blushes at this point and stares down into her tea cup. Still half full, she picks it up and swallows a large mouthful before pushing her chair back and standing up suddenly.
"I really should be off. Thank you so much for the tea and biscuits."

Dropping a five pound note on the table, Diana hurries back out the way she came, leaving the elderly woman sitting alone at the table looking rather confused.

CHAPTER THIRTY FOUR

A hush falls over the happy chatter of the mosque as one by one people notice Diana. Arriving at a busy time of the day, she cannot slip in practically unnoticed as she had managed to do in the church earlier on. Taking a deep breath, Diana holds her head high and pushes her shoulders back before smiling and waving at the people gawking at her. Making her way forward her smile spreads wider across her face as the Imam comes forward, his arms outstretched in greeting

"My lady, it is so good to see you again."

He kisses both her cheeks, before stepping back and admiring her from arms length

"You look well. Please, join me for some tea?"

Diana nods her consent and follows him out of the room, smiling apologetically at the people gathered there. It takes a few moments for the silence left by her arrival to abate, but when it does the room explodes with excited chatter. Laughing, the Imam who has escorted Diana out closes the door and offers by way of explanation

"Many of them thought that your presence on previous occasions was just a rumour. They're excited to find out that it was true."

Diana blushes and sits elegantly down in the seat offered to her and begins with an apology

"I'm sorry I haven't been visiting as much recently......"

Diana's apology wears off as the Imam waves his hand
"It does not matter. What matters is that you are here now. But no Dodi or Kamil today?"

Diana smiles
"Dodi is working and Kamil is with his nanny. I wanted some time to myself for a little bit."

The conversation is interrupted as a pot of tea and a plate of biscuits are placed down on the table between the two. Diana smiles by way of thank you as a cup is poured for her and helps herself to a chocolate digestive. She leans back in her chair
"I'm sure you can understand that things have been hard for me, a lot of things have been said about me being here. Some good and some bad. It's taken me a while to realise that all that matters is what I think."

Both Diana and the Imam seem surprised by her frankness and her words hang in the air for some time as they both sip their tea in silence. Diana fiddles with her teaspoon, staring at it intently as she speaks again
"I know that all Dodi, and my boys, want for me is for me to be happy. There is no pressure there. However, I can't deny that it would make Dodi and his family so much happier if I were to convert. And despite what they say, I think William and Harry would be much happier if I didn't. Of course, the rest of the royal family would be infinitely happier if I didn't convert as well, but their views are of no importance to me now. I've done my time towing the royal line."

Diana seems to have forgotten that she is not alone, all her thoughts, fears and concerns tumbling out of her as if she is weighing up her decisions.

"I mean, it's not like I go to church all that often or anything. I certainly don't spend time reading the bible. I try to be the sort of person a good Christian is expected to be, but I think that's just being a good person in general. Just because you're not a Christian doesn't mean you're not a good person. I got married in a church, that didn't have any bearing on the type of marriage it was though. William and Harry were christened and they're both good Christian boys. Kamil's a good boy and he hasn't been christened. Dodi is a good man and he wasn't christened. And however we decide to get married, that marriage will be what we make of it. It shouldn't matter where we do it. It doesn't matter where we do it."

Diana leans forward and picks up her cup of tea, catching sight of the Imam sitting in front of her and staring as if she had forgotten he is there. Absorbed in the pattern on his tea cup, he does his best to seem as if he has not been listening to Diana's ramblings. She blushes deep red

"I'm so sorry! You don't need me here talking to myself like some sort of lunatic. I'll go."

Diana puts down her cup and begins to rise out of her seat, but the Imam puts up his hand to stop her. Pausing mid way to a standing position, Diana stares at him as he speaks

"You came here for time to think. Please, sit down. If you want to talk, then I am here to listen and I can assure you that anything you say will not pass outside of these four walls. If you want me to leave you to think in peace then I am more than happy to do that also."

Diana sits back down in her seat and stares at the man in front of her. A question blurts out from her lips as if by accident

"Am I the right sort of woman to be a Muslim?"

The Imam smiles briefly before a cloud seems to pass over his face.

"Those people that were shown on the television are a disgrace. Islam is about enlightenment and bringing the words of the Prophet Mohammad, peace be upon him, to the world. It is not about picking and choosing who should receive that enlightenment, but about offering it to all that are willing to learn."

He looks to Diana's face, his words seeming to have little effect on her. He speaks in a softer tone

"I am sure that it must have been difficult to hear so much negativity, to feel that you were being publicly vilified. I am more than sure that there are two, three times as many Muslims who are thrilled to welcome you into the community. I personally cannot think of anyone more suited to the Muslim life. Charity is such a big part of Islam, and you have already done such wonderful work for so many different charities, simply because you wanted to. Because you knew that it was the right thing to do. That makes you a very special person."

He reaches out across the table and takes Diana's hand, ignoring the tears that are slipping down her cheeks. Diana clutches his hand tightly in return, avoiding his gaze as the tears continue to fall. Removing himself from his chair, the Imam creeps swiftly across the room, returning with a box of tissues almost before Diana has noticed that he is gone. He does not offer her his hand again, instead holding out the box of tissues almost like a barrier between them. Diana takes several, dabbing at her cheeks before blowing her nose noisily

"Thank you. I'm so sorry. You must think terribly of me, turning up here and telling you all my problems before bursting into tears."

The Imam smiles kindly and once again offers Diana the box of tissues without speaking. Diana sniffs twice, before looking up and imploring with wet eyes

"How am I supposed to work out what I want for me when what everyone else wants is so intertwined with my happiness?"

"That is a question that people have been trying to answer for a long time. You cannot please all of the people all of the time..."

Diana smiles warmly at the well known phrase

"...but I think in most people's case, making a decision for purely selfish reasons rarely brings happiness either."

Standing up, the Imam takes hold of Diana's hand and clasps it tightly

"I have things that I must attend to. You are welcome to stay here as long as you need to. Talk to people, I think you will find that it helps."

He lets go of her hand and smiles down at her, before turning and walking out of the room. Diana picks up her cup of tea and takes a delicate sip, before grimacing and putting it down again. Pushing back her chair, Diana stands up and begins to move slowly around the room. Posters of famous quotations line the walls, attributed to many different people. Copies of the Qur'an are placed conveniently on several tables, pages marked and covers worn from usage. Diana picks up a photograph from on top of one of the many bookcases, smiling widely at the eclectic mix of age gathered in the shot. Elderly men and women smile alongside children and their parents, several babies are held close in their mother's arms. Diana places the photograph carefully back down on the shelf and continues to walk around the room, before making her way to the door. Pausing at the threshold, Diana moves out into the main room, the weight of hundreds of pairs of eyes on her.

It is late afternoon when Diana leaves the mosque, her step is light and there is a smile on her face. The air is still warm and Diana throws her jacket over her arm as she walks to the car that is waiting for her. Without waiting for the door to be opened for her, she heaves herself into the four by four and throws her jacket and bag on the seat next to her. Beaming at the driver, Diana straps herself in before requesting

"Could you take me home please?"

The driver, who has not yet acknowledged Diana's presence, does not reply. The faint noise of the radio filters through to the back of the car and Diana's smile slowly begins to fade from her face, replaced by a look of annoyance. She leans forward and taps the driver on the shoulder

"I'm ready to go home."

The driver turns and looks at Diana as if seeing her for the first time. His face is ashen and his eyes are wide. Diana waves her hand in front of his face

"Can you hear me?"

Turning his had back round to face the front of the car, the driver still makes no move to start the engine, instead leaning forward and turning up the radio. Leaning further forward in frustration, all signs of her previous happy mood gone, Diana snaps

"I've had a long and frankly very enlightening day. If it's not too much trouble for you I'd like to get home and talk to my fiancé about it."

Turning back around to stare at her, the driver opens his mouth to respond but seems unable to form the words. Diana unclips her seat belt and begins to move forwards in the car as if to try and get closer to the driver in an attempt to make him understand her better. As she crouches next to the drivers seat the words coming from the radio seem to reach her for the first time

"The United States is in a state of shock after a day of attacks which have left thousands dead and New York's World Trade Centre destroyed. American Airlines Flight 11 was hijacked at 8.25 Eastern Daylight Time and 18 minutes later crashed into the north tower of the World Trade Center."

Diana's mouth falls open in disbelief. She reaches out to adjust the volume on the radio, turning it up in an attempt to hear better.

"United Airlines Flight 175 - which had been hijacked within minutes of the first plane - was flown into the south tower at 9.03 Eastern Daylight Time causing another devastating explosion.

At 9.40 Eastern Daylight Time a third hijacked airliner - American Airlines Flight 77 - was flown into the side of the Pentagon in Washington."

Diana's hand raises to her open mouth in shock as the woman on the radio continues

"It is believed that the Muslim extremist group Al-Qaeda is responsible for the attacks, which have so far killed more than three thousand people."

Slumping back to her seat, Diana stares at the mosque she has just left, the joyful hubbub and noise of the people gathered there spilling out into the street. The details of death and destruction seep from the radio as people file out from the mosque, laughing and waving warmly at Diana, frozen in shock in the back seat of her car.